GOLDENGROVE

Goldengrove, originally published in 1972, takes its title (as does its sequel, *Unleaving*) from lines by Gerard Manley Hopkins – *Margaret, are you grieving/Over Goldengrove unleaving?* – in his poem 'Spring and Fall'. Both books are set in a house in Cornwall much loved by the children who visit it, and the author has revealed that this was her grandmother's house in St Ives, where, as a young child evacuated from the dangers of war-time London, she was intensely happy. What she did not realize – until she began to write *Goldengrove* and found the story obstinately refusing to be written in any but the present tense – was that Virginia Woolf had also lived in St Ives and had also looked out at the bay and its lighthouse. So the echoes of Virginia Woolf's writing reviewers found in *Goldengrove* seem to have their origins in the powerful influence of a particular place.

Jill Paton Walsh was born in London in 1937, and was educated at a convent and St Anne's College, Oxford. After her marriage in 1961, and the birth of her first child, she began to write as an escape 'from the boredom of being trapped in a small house with a baby that could not yet talk'. Her first book, *Hengest's Tale*, a historical novel, was published in 1966: her subsequent books have each been different, as she developed her literary gifts in different ways. She won the Whitbread Award for *The Emperor's Winding Sheet* (1974), the Boston Globe-Horn Book Award for *Unleaving* (1976) and the Universe fiction prize for *A Parcel of Patterns* (1983).

D0229550

GOLDENGROVE

Jill Paton Walsh

THE BODLEY HEAD
LONDON SYDNEY
TORONTO

British Library Cataloguing
in Publication Data
Paton Walsh, Jill
Goldengrove. —(Bodley bookshelf)
I. Title
823'.914 [F] PR6066.A84
ISBN 0–370–30630–9

Copyright © Jill Paton Walsh 1972
All rights reserved
Printed and bound in Finland for
The Bodley Head Ltd
9 Bow Street, London WC2E 7AL
by Werner Söderström Oy

First published by Macmillan London Ltd 1972
This edition first published by The Bodley Head Ltd 1985

For Marni

Rhythmically, like a runner, the train gasps and pants as it pulls up the long rise. Hearing its heavy breathing, looking at azalea, and rhododendron, and gloriously improbable palm trees growing wild along the verges of the line, the passengers can tell that they are nearly there. Sitting near the end of the train, looking and looking through the window – it has made his nose dirty – for the moment when the line turns suddenly and you can see the sea, Paul knows it is nearly there. Madge is somewhere, looking for it too, Paul tells himself. Somewhere in the snake of carriages ahead, she is riding, looking for the sea. They get me to the train in time, just in time, for Daddy to kiss me once, on my left cheek, and for me to just leap into the last carriage as the train draws breath, and the platform starts to jerk sideways. They are so jumpy they can hardly bear to wait to slam the door on me. And it's always a non-corridor train, I suppose it has to be a thin train to fit through the tunnels or something, and so here we always are, together and apart, going there together, and meeting when we get there. Of course, my people don't want to meet her people, that's why it is, of course. . . .

"There it is!" he interrupts himself, for now the train is turning, and suddenly the sea is there, Oh, wider than you ever expect though of course, thinks Paul, I know it is, and a fantastic blue, like the ultra-marine in my paintbox when I first touch the brush over it and wet it, and all frisky with windy white horses galloping shorewards to smash and leap on the broken, black, rocky, petering-out-here edges of the land. So round we go now, running at the foot of the cliff, beneath Goldengrove, with white puffs of smoke ascending to signal in the garden to Gran that we are coming, and as we come, just here – yes, there it is! – we can see the lighthouse in the bay.

Getting up, Paul pulls his holdall down from the luggage rack, steadying his rocking body in the diddlidum swaying of the train.

Madge, looking through the window, leaning her head back into the crown of her straw hat, thinks about Paul. I suppose he's on the train somewhere. I suppose he nearly missed it again. He's awfully bad at catching things. Except fish. We'll see the lighthouse soon. She looks for it. There it is in the bay, standing on its rocky island. It is a cleft island, through which, when the ocean is angry, the white surf surges and boils, but today the sea is only playing. She looks at it, and names it to herself. Godrevy . . . Godrevy . . . a dream upon the waters . . . no, that's Byron on Venice. No wonder I got through that exam. I've got a really English examination mind, through and through. And it's all very well being fussed over, and being hurried forwards, and being the youngest girl they've ever let take Matric, but I wonder if it marks you for life? I mean will I wake up when I'm married saying "Busy old fool, unruly sun (Donne)" to myself? Will I always be quoting in my head, and telling myself where the line comes from? Oh, hell! I won't think school yet, it's still holiday for a while.

And we're nearly there. I got here, in spite of it all. It's always the same; they always try to stop me.

Always take me off somewhere else, and say it's instead of coming here. And then they try to fix it so I won't be here at the same time as Paul. "You can go if you really must," says Mother, coldly. "But it will have to be in July. We are going to Berne in August." I wonder what it's all about, I really do. She *will* ask about Paul, and then whatever I say she hates it, and gets all upset . . . but I'm here now, or nearly, and it will be the same as ever. That's the thing about Goldengrove, it's always the same as ever . . . though I suppose it will be different this time because of being later in the year. "If you had gone in July, as I suggested," Mother said, "you wouldn't have had to miss the beginning of term."

"Miss Higgins said I had to read widely for the sixth form curriculum," I said, "and I could do that anywhere." It had to be September, because that's when Paul could come. But September is the only difference there will be to Goldengrove, which is always the same. Can the time of year cast a difference over everything?

The train jolts to a halt, and lets out a long dying sigh of steam. Madge gets up, allows the elderly gentleman who got into her carriage at St Erth to lift down her suitcase for her, and gets out. The bright-smelling sea air washes over her, and she raises a swift hand to hold onto her hat. Running from the back of the train, leaning sideways to counterbalance his bulging holdall, hopping in and out dodging the other passengers, Paul is hurtling towards her, shouting "Madge!" and eyes shining.

At Goldengrove their grandmother sits in the garden in a wicker chair on the terrace, with the windows behind her open to the drifts of lavender

9

ringing the lawn. The seven beech trees and five
chestnuts after which her house is named lie to the
right of the grounds, with a September colour just
creeping over them. In front of her the lawns slope
away to the rose garden, and, beyond, the land drops
steeply to the garden wall, with the little gate to the
path to the beach, to the sea. She hears the train
striving, chuff, chuff, below the garden, and sees
cotton-wool puffs of cloud rising from behind the
roses and dispersing through the garden, bringing
a sudden smutty smell to interrupt the lavender for
a moment. They are here, she thinks, my dear Madge
and Paul, together. Their parents make me so angry
. . . no, I won't think of that. They are here now.
Amy has sent Mr Arthur to fetch them up to the
house in the car. I shall have their fresh young faces,
their bright smiles around me now for a little while.

"I have put you in the best spare bedroom this
year, Madge," says Gran, when the kissing on the
doorstep has been done. To Paul's crestfallen face
she says, "You are getting too big to share a room,
you know. Look how big you are, Paul! You've
grown six inches since last year." But standing up
against the notched door-frame in the kitchen shows
it to be not more than two inches, really. The tea
tray is ready on the scrubbed deal table in the
kitchen, and, while Gran is measuring Madge, Paul
manages to stuff home three of the paste and
cucumber sandwiches. The cake plate looks too
finely balanced to steal from. Madge isn't much
taller. It's round her middle somewhere Gran ought
to measure her, thinks Paul, looking at Madge
critically. It's somewhere there she's gone different.
Narrower, and bendy-looking.

"Oh, Paul, dear!" cries Gran, looking at the in-roads on the sandwiches. "And you haven't washed your hands from the train yet!"

Upstairs, with her suitcase open on the foot of the bed, Madge is trying the best spare room. It doesn't look towards the sea, she finds, but into the trees. It is large and square, with long windows, and a dressing-table. Thoughtfully, she puts her hair-brush down on a lace mat. She is divided, partly trying in a pleased way what it feels like to be a best spare person, with glazed chintz curtains, and a moon-shaped mirror, and lots of mats and little boxes beneath it laid out ready – what for? – and roses in a silver bowl beside the bed. But part of her is sick with disappointment, because it is not the same, after all, as every year till now, and there will be no whispering to Paul from under the starched arc of sheet raised by her thin shoulder as she lies facing him across the room, not seeing him in the bedtime, lights-out-now-dears of Gran's attic.

Madge throws her clothes out of the suitcase, and pushes them hastily into the drawers, empty except for little muslin bags of dusty dried lavender. She doesn't bother to hang anything up. She sits down on the bed. What is it about Paul I like, anyway? she asks herself. He makes me feel like doing the last pieces of a jigsaw puzzle, or that time I mended the Worcester cup Mother broke, he makes me feel that things are where they ought to be, in their right place. But it's stupid of me, really it is, he's only a boy after all, and younger than me. It would be much more fun if he were older. She imagines to herself a scene at the school garden-party, in which Sophia, the snobbiest girl in the fifth can be heard

11

saying "*Who* is the handsome boy you were talking to?" and Madge says, "Oh that's my cousin, Paul. He's taking me to the dance tonight!" But then she sees at once that if he were older, and likely to take her to a dance, there would have been no long sandy days playing with the boat on the beach down there, and her disappointment wins and she races up the stairs to the attic to talk to Paul.

"Will anyone have remembered to put the boat out for us?" says Paul, looking down towards the sea.

"I don't know. Now it's Amy, instead of Mrs Arthur, perhaps not. It was Mrs Arthur who always remembered."

"Mr Arthur still does the garden though. Perhaps he'll have thought of it."

"Tell you what, though, Paul, if anyone has remembered at all they're sure to remember to forbid us to put it in the water."

"Worse luck!"

"Oh, I don't know," says Madge. "It probably would be dangerous. And it's fun to play with anyhow." And they stand for a moment, looking pleased to be here at each other.

The attic is painted white, with sloping angled ceilings, and a big dormer window, with a window-seat beneath it, that fills the room with a view of the sea. Madge casts a rueful glance at the patchwork counterpane of the bed that is not now hers, and the funny bamboo bookcase with only Paul's things laid on it, and then goes to sit on the window-seat, and watch the view. And from here she sees the sweep of the bay, and dark Godrevy with its white tower of a lighthouse, and looking the other way the harbour, with the town around it, and behind the harbour the domed grassy hill called the Island, for island it once was, before the fishermen's houses edged out along the sand bar to reach it, so Gran says. It is green below the little chapel on top, and squared with white sheets stretched out to dry and bleach. Nearer lies the long golden beach with the little railway line behind it – the beach that has bathing huts made of coloured canvas, and always lots of people on it, and is quite unlike their beach, which is small and lonely, for the only way down to it lies over Gran's land, and so it is their very own.

"Look, Madge," says Paul, coming to sit beside her on the sun-faded cover of the window-seat. "There's a wisp of smoke from over the trees. Someone must be in Gran's cottage."

But looking, Madge cannot see it, and the brassy noise of the tea-gong tells them that new, redhaired Amy is carrying the tea-tray out to the terrace, and they race down the stairs.

Gran is sitting in her chair, pouring tea, with a shawl spread over her knees. "What's that for, Gran?" Paul asks her.

"I feel the cold so, nowadays," she says, while Madge taking her place in a deck chair, feels only the sun.

"It's warm," says Paul.

"I'm all skin and bone these days," says Gran.

After tea Madge says, "Let's go and look for strawberries in the wood." But Paul says, "Let's go to the beach."

Bother, why can't he want what I want? thinks Madge, crossly. "I want to look for strawberries first," she says.

"There won't *be* any in September, will there,

Gran?" says Paul, but Gran has gently dozed off to sleep in the sun which she declared only a moment ago was not enough to keep her warm.

Off goes Paul at a run, down through the rose garden, to the garden gate, to the path, to the beach. Madge walks into the grove that gives the house its name, thinking: it is just beginning to turn gold, and I have never seen it gold before, only green, always green, hundreds of variously-lit little floating boats of green and lizard-spotted light. Below these trees, especially here round the huge chestnut tree – I was here once when it was in flower, like huge candles – the wild strawberries grow. They spread like wild-fire, Gran says. They all come from six plants Grandfather put here once, long ago when he was alive, Gran says. And I want to eat some, I want them to be here, I don't want it to be September and I shall hate my mother for *ten years* if there aren't any just because trying to keep me from Paul she made it be September instead of August, and I didn't like Berne anyway! Well, not much. Oh, strawberries, be here!

Miraculously, the strawberries are still there. Not many; not like full summer, when the little plants are speckled scarlet that you can see at a glance, and Mr Arthur can go out for an hour and bring back a bowlful for dessert, even though it takes heaven knows how many to fill a kitchen bowl, and there are enough even though Madge and Paul have been happy with mouth and fingers stained with them for hours beneath the trees the day before. Now Madge has to look and look, gently turning the leaves, and finds them one by one, few, late, and last ones. They are no bigger than her little finger-nail, as though they were for fairies, and they taste

14

very delicate and clear, like an ordinary strawberry, she thinks, just after you've eaten it, when you are full of the pleased feeling, and your tongue remembers it. "I shall find twelve before I go in," says Madge, aloud.

Paul is standing on the beach, looking out to sea. You can see the lighthouse from here, but not the harbour, nor the house, nor the trees of Goldengrove. But behind him rises a grassy, wild-flowered slope, rather steep, with a little path descending diagonally; to his left and right the cliff becomes steeper and rocky, and in a broken staircase steps down to run out as a rocky promentary into the dancing sea. A half-moon of sand lies between. A little cove, with no name, and why should it need one, for it is private; it is Gran's, though she never comes down here now. The path is too much for her, she says.

The boat is there, he sees, his first moment down there, but not because it has been remembered, he sees next moment, but because it has been forgotten. No one put it away after last year; no one heaved and hauled it up the path to the shed at the bottom of the garden, and it is half full of sand, and swathed in seaweed, and tied up to a ring in the rock with a rusty chain. Paul decides to leave playing with it till Madge comes. Instead he takes off his shoes and socks, and walks in the surf, jumping in the bolsters of froth, but keeping clear of the great hills of green, white-crested water, rolling in, smoking as they break, for the sea is high here, being ocean, and having come a long way; "A long fetch, these waves have," said Jeremy the boatman last year. They are high enough to knock you down, and drag you under, thinks Paul. And it's cold, I'm feeling it too, in this thin shirt flecked with sea-water, and a small cloud crossing the sinking sun. Time to go in.

In the garden again he meets Madge. "I found some," she says.

"Don't believe you!"

"Smell them!" she says, and opening a purple-pink cavern of mouth full of white teeth and arched tongue, she breathes strawberry breath in his face, enough to make him feel jealous.

"I'll find more than you tomorrow!" he says. "The boat's there. It's been left out."

"Still in one piece?"

"More or less. I didn't look till you came."

"Tomorrow," she says.

Now the little glasses of tonic wine, and the dish of raisins and almonds, and a radio symphony concert turned down low to go with their Grandmother's evening gossip will come next, before bed, and tomorrow.

In darkness Madge wakes up, hearing her bad dreams. A storm has blown up since nightfall, and wind and rain now rattle on the shut panes of glass. The curtain bellies and tugs in front of the window she has opened; as she props herself on one arm the wind sucks it out through the window into the rain. She runs to close it, and finds it jammed. A gale of cold air clutches her nightdress round her as she pulls. The sky outside is black and broken silver with storm and moon. Gran comes in, holding a lamp. She cries, "Oh dear, my dear, you'll catch your death!" and with surprising force – she looks so frail now – she closes the window.

"I'm going to close Paul's now," she says. "Come and look out to sea, Madge. My eyes do let me down so." Madge follows her.

Paul's window is shut already. He has not woken up, and only a hump in the bed and the familiar tuft of hair sunk in the pillow can be seen of him by the lamp in Gran's hand. Madge looks out to sea, and sees patchy, interrupted moonlight on dark tossing water.

"Are there any ships there?" says Gran, in a low voice, not to wake Paul.

"I can't see any Gran," says Madge, and I don't think I'd see them from here even if there were any, she thinks. They'd show like a shadow on the water at most, a black patch among all these shifting blacknesses.

"Won't they all be in the harbour?" she whispers. The wind sounds fiercely up here, whistling on the roof tiles, and keening down the drainpipes of the house.

"The Frenchmen won't, dear," says Gran. "Can you see no lights in the bay?"

"Only Godrevy light, Gran."

"All's well, then. Come down," and they go down, closing the attic door gently on sleeping Paul.

"Why wouldn't they be in the harbour, Gran?" asks Madge, at her bedroom door.

"It's the French trawlermen, Madge dear. The war stopped them coming, but they're back again these last few years. They don't know this coast well enough. They come round Land's End, looking for

17

shelter, and the bay here looks safe enough. They don't want to pay harbour dues. And then, well, there's no love lost between them and the local men. The men here say the foreigners use fine-mesh nets, and ruin the fishing for others. So the Frenchmen drop anchor in the bay, and when the wind gets up northeasterly, that's not good enough. Sometimes someone goes out to them, to warn them, and try to make them come in, but they don't always heed it."

"What happens then?"

"They can drag their anchors, poor fellows, and run onto the rocks. Every year, somewhere hereabouts, a few men lost. A trawler on the rocks, or a man washed overboard. Such a pity; such a waste. But when they're in trouble they show lights, or send up flares. You would have seen something. The lifeboat goes out to them. But there's nothing amiss tonight," and I mustn't frighten her, thinks Gran. I shouldn't have let her see I was concerned. "All's well tonight," she repeats. "Sleep well, Madge."

So back to the now cold hollowed bed, and listen to the wind again, closed out by the four walls of the house, and Madge sleeps without knowing she has slept, till she opens her eyes again on the bright morning shining all round the room. Finding where she is she wakes thinking first "Not Goldengrove!" and then, Oh, yes it is, it is, it is Goldengrove's best spare room, and Paul waking up without me up another flight of stairs, and perhaps it is after all better to sit up – she sits up – and stretch – she stretches – than to double-up winded and fighting while Paul jumps on my tummy to wake me! Getting dressed she stares briefly at her naked reflection framed like a Regency portrait in a round of mirror, for it has not escaped Madge's own attention that she is changing somehow around the middle, and she keeps a regular eye on herself to see how she is shaping up. Looking out she sees that Paul is up and out already – she can see his tracks marked in the dew on the lawn.

No mackerel for breakfast today, for the fishing fleet, says Gran, stayed safely tucked up in the harbour last night, and Paul who slept through every sound of it, and slept through Gran walking with a lamp in her hand, trembling at the thought of death in the watery darkness, clearly thinks that the storm cannot have been excuse enough to miss the sweet firm pink and grey flesh flaking off the web of thin translucent bones on his morning plate. Amy has provided kippers instead, and I like kippers quite a lot, thinks Paul, but they're not the same because we eat them at home, and mackerel only here. And I've brought my six spinners in a chipped blue metal box, and a pair of lines, and Jeremy will take me fishing in his boat, and I will let Madge have the red and silver spinner which always catches the largest fish, and we will bring mackerel gleaming, hanging by the gills in a loop of string, for Amy to cook. I will carry them, and they will brush against my bare leg all the way, and leave a shiny scaly patch on me, like a terrible skin disease, which will wash off in the bath. He grins to himself.

"Nice kipper, dearie?" says Gran.

"Fine, thanks, Gran," and, "Do hurry up, Madge. We'll be late down to the beach," says Paul.

"How can we be late," asks Madge, "when there isn't a time we should be there by?"

"We ought to be there as soon as we can!" says Paul.

"Well, it isn't as soon as we can yet, because I can't eat any quicker than I am eating," says Madge. "Gran, is there anything we can do to help in the house before we go out?"

If I asked her to pick roses and put them in bowls for me, thinks Gran, they would stay a little. I would watch them going to and fro from bed to bed, and bringing the flowers in. But they would rather be gone. Paul is so eager he can hardly sit still. "No thank you, Madge," she says. "Nothing this morning. Another day perhaps."

And at once the children are up and away, through the open French windows to the terrace, and over the lawn, and out of sight though their voices rise up to her like birds' voices from the path below. She smiles over the half-drunk coffee cups and the kipper bones.

"The beach felt different last night," says Paul to Madge, as they run down the path, dead-nettle and Ragged Robin leaning to brush against their legs all the way.

"How different?" asks Madge.

"I didn't feel alone there," he says.

As he says it they are there, leaping from the little platform of squared stones that once made a mooring, or a landing-stage, at the foot of the path, and landing ankles-under in soft sand that slides on their dry skins like silk, and rises to every puff of wind. One or two steps further, and a dry black crackly line of seaweed marks the top of the tide, like the lacy edge of an old black petticoat, and beyond it the width of the beach is golden sand, firm with the sea, that holds every toe-mark, every battlement of a sandcastle, Paul remembers, and they run across it hand in hand to go surf-hopping in the eternal rolling coming-and-going edge of the sea.

In a little while they are both wet through. I always mean to be careful till I get my dress off, thinks Madge, and I never am, and I never learn, and I'm not sorry. She peels off her wet dress, and drops it in the sand, thinking, I'll spread it on a rock to dry in a minute. Paul is putting his shorts and aertex shirt to dry on a rock straight away. Like her he has his swimming things on underneath the accident-prone top layer, and then they are back in the water. Playing in the waves like a dolphin Madge once saw in a documentary film – how sleek and wet and shiny, and supple and intelligent they were, Paul reminds her – Paul simply thinks sea. Pull back, foaming, gather, rise, break, crash in white waterfalls! he thinks. Run, jump, swim in that one, oh, there's a high one, can I stand steady in that one? No, help! Here I go, head-under, struggling, and come up with my hair full of sand, and gritty trickles, oh it tastes of salt! running down my face.

"Are you all right, Paul?" calls Madge, over the waves.

"No! Drowned, drowned!" he shouts back, and not seeing the big wave come, goes under again. He rises to Madge, wading, struggling with deep heavy legs towards him. Seeing him all right she pretends at once that she was only coming to chase him, but he knows. "Fusspot!" he calls.

Later they lie in the soft sand to dry, and look at the great cloud-castles wheeling by, and the gulls drifting circles in the depths of the sky. "You are right about it feeling different, Paul," says Madge. "I feel watched."

21

"There's nobody here," he says. "Shall we look at the boat now?"

"Yes, now," Madge says. We always have to come round to it slowly, she thinks, I wonder why. It has something to do with liking it so much. I don't understand me.

The boat lies tilted slightly, slightly submerged in the sand. Sand has washed inside it, and settled there, giving it a smooth beachy floor. Its sides are festooned with the necklace-of-beads sort of sea-weed that pops when you squeeze its bubbles. Lower down it is livid with the bright green weedy slime that covers the sea-washed rocks. And yet it is all in one piece, and still riding on its rusty chain, though it is the slope of the beach it rides now, not the tilting sea. But the winter has left its mark. Most of the boat is bleached grey, weathered down. Deep cracks run along every grain of the once living wood, and it has a pale worn smoothness, like leprosy. Running fingers over it finds ups and downs like bones. A little paint still holds on it. It was turquoise blue paint, all crazed along the cracks in the wood, and mostly flaked away, so that what remains are little lines of it, curling at the edges, and bright against the pale wood. Madge scratches at the raised edge of a piece with her fingernail, and at once the whole flake lifts off.

"Could we paint it blue again, Paul?" she asks.

"We'd have to empty all the sand out, and scrape off all the seaweed," he says. "The bottom will be rotten as hell with all this wet sand in it, but we could paint the upper bit blue again. It would be as good as ever to play in."

"Let's. Let's paint it just exactly that blue-green,

green-blue colour it must have been when it was new. I'd like that."

"Girls!" says Paul. "Paint your boat sky-blue-pink, this year's fashion colour!" Madge punches him in the ribs, and he continues cheerfully, "We could paint it. It would be a lot of work before we got to the coloured bit. You'd jolly well have to help."

"I don't want to start today," says Madge. "I feel watched."

"Yes," Paul says. "And now I know who's doing it. Look up there, Madge!"

Looking up she follows his pointing finger. On the cliff overlooking the cove is Gran's cottage – a little, low, snuggling-into-the-slope, white-washed, slate-roofed, tiny house, a fisherman's once, then the servants' in the days when Goldengrove had more hands than Amy's to run it, before the war, that time which the adults all remember so much, and the children hardly at all. The trees mask the cottage from the house, and it looks out to sea, with a path of its own branching from the other path, and a crazy cliff-top garden that is walled for safety and where only sea-pinks grow. Only from here can the cove be seen. And in the garden of the cottage a man is sitting and staring at them.

"What cheek!" says Madge, indignantly.

"Of course," says Paul, very slowly, in his voice of lordly anger, "Gran must have rented the cottage to him. So, therefore, he has every right to *be* up there, in his garden. But he jolly well doesn't have to spend all his time *staring* at us!"

"He'll have to stop, or he'll spoil our beach for us!"

"I'll make him stop," says Paul. "All we have to do is stare back."

23

"Well, we have been," says Madge. "He must have seen by now that we've stopped playing, and are standing here side by side, looking at him. And he's still looking straight at us."

Paul jumps up and down and waves his arms. He puts his thumbs in his ears, and waggles his spread-eagled fingers. Joining in, Madge thumbs her nose vigorously at the distant figure. Unflinchingly, and without moving at all, he continues to fix her in his gaze. Perhaps he *isn't* looking at us, she thinks, but what else can he be doing, just sitting there like that? She turns round to see the thing behind her that might be drawing his eyes. Nothing but sand and rock. It *is* us! she thinks, exasperated. "Yah!" she yells at him, fists clenched. "*Stare cat, stare cat, whatdye think yer looking at!*" but her derisive chanting falls short of him, at his distance, lost in sea and bird calls. Paul picks up his spade, and begins to run, trailing it at an angle behind him, scratching huge wobbly letters in the sand. BUZZ OFF he writes, SCRAM! Madge takes a stick and writes SPY! LOOK AWAY. THIS BEACH IS PRIVATE runs Paul. There is hardly any smooth sand left to scrawl upon, and they stand, out of breath, panting, and looking up, and still, over the low stone wall of his garden, they can see the man staring at them, steadily.

"Come on, Madge," says Paul. "I'm going to spy on *him*, and see how *he* likes it!"

She runs after him. They scramble up the path, doubled-over as they run, so that they are hidden as in a tunnel by the encroaching flowery weeds. Madge's heart is beating, as though she were playing hide-and-seek, or "It". The clever children, good at catching spies who have eluded the police, the brave dauntless children who capture dangerous criminals single-handed – not that she has ever met any, but she has read about them – come back to her, and she tries them on for size. She begins to laugh. Looking back, Paul lays a hushing finger over his answering grin.

They run past the gate to Gran's garden, and on, further along the path. It takes them to the front of the cottage, or rather to the front door, which nestles in a sprawl of overblown roses in the side of the little house. The door is standing open. Ducking down again, Paul leads the way round the outside of the garden wall. It is only some three feet high, so they have to stalk, still doubled-over, Indian fashion. The wall is nearly at the edge of the cliff, and the grass they are creeping on slopes dangerously, and then drops away altogether to the rocks below. Every few yards as they go, Paul bobs up to spy on the staring man, and when he does so, Madge does too. The man is sitting – they can see his back – in a wooden garden chair. A dog lies on the grass beside him, a black Labrador. The dog's front legs are stretched out very straight and crossed one over the other; he looks as though he had just keeled over sideways from standing up, and lain there. He is asleep, sun-drunk, but still has one black ear cocked towards them. They move, and his ear lifts. They stand still, and very slowly the ear subsides again. But what is the man doing? wonders Madge, for surely he is still staring at the beach, and we are gone from there. She looks down, and sees the scrawled words written in the sand. They edge further round the wall. Next time they bob up she can see he has a book on his knee. But he isn't looking at it! she tells herself. He isn't even pretending to read it, thinks Paul. "Madge!

25

Madge," he hisses, waiting for her to wriggle up to him, and breathing urgently in her ear, "I vote we work round to just in front of him, and then stand up suddenly, and just stare back. Don't flinch, don't speak." They hear the dog growling sleepily, like an undecided snore, and he hastily finishes, "Just give him a bellyful of what he's giving us, right?"

"Right," murmurs Madge, though I am not very good at staring, she thinks. Jenny Martin can out-stare me any day of the week. She wriggles further and further along behind Paul. The grass margin they are on grows narrower, and the grass is that fine and only-beside-the-sea kind that is round and fine, like hair, and very slippery. I hope it's soon, thinks Madge. Oh, Paul be careful!

Paul stands up suddenly. She stands up, too. Dog cocks his ear. They face the man, and stare straight into his wide-open eyes. Steadily he stares back at them. It takes Madge a long second to understand what is wrong. She is looking at a man with dark hair slightly grey at the temples, wearing an open-necked shirt. A book lies open on his knees, and he does not look at it. His hands are held out straight over the page, fingers downwards, like a piano-player's. His fingertips travel steadily, brushing the paper. His head is held rather high, like a man looking at the distance, but when Madge and Paul pop up right in front of him, his eyes do not change focus at all. In the brilliant sunlight of mid-day he turns skywards eyes so dilated that you cannot see what colour they are at all. And oh, he isn't staring, thinks Madge, oh poor man, poor man, he's blind, and we are wicked, wicked, to have mocked and jeered and ambushed him!

"Is there anybody there?" says the man, but how does he know, Paul wonders, since we've been so quiet the dog hasn't even woken, only rumbled a bit, and my shadow doesn't fall as far as where he is sitting? "Who's there?" says the man more sharply. Nobody answers.

But overcome with remorse, Madge grabs at Paul to pull him away, and he slips, and she grips onto him, and goes too. Silently they fall together from the grassy ledge, and hit another tuft of grass, and then another, and then they are not quite falling, but hurtling from one bump to another on the way down. They find themselves lying on a grass-topped outcrop half way down, clinging together, gasping. "Are you all right?" and "Are you all right?" they ask, but it seems to be only bruises. "Could have been nasty, though," says Paul.

"Can we climb down from here?" asks Madge, but it looks as if they can. Overhead the blind man's dog, woken at last, is barking. "Who's there?" he shouts.

Slithering down and down they reach the beach. At once Madge begins to run, scuffing the letters on the sand with her heels and toes, rubbing them out.

"What are you doing that for?" asks Paul.

"Oh, it's horrid of us," says Madge.

"But he can't see it," Paul says.

"He wasn't staring at all," says Madge, shuffling round the great S of SPY with tears in her eyes.

"He wasn't seeing, but he jolly well was staring," says Paul, and, "Come on Madge, we'll make the lunch late for Gran if you don't come now."

Madge hasn't remembered her dress, of course, till the moment she needs it again, so she has to go home clammy and crumpled, and scratchy with clinging sand.

"The beach again now, dearies?" says Gran over her coffee cup. Madge glances swiftly at Paul. "I thought I might pick some flowers and arrange them for you, Gran," says Madge, because, she thinks, I certainly don't want to go back there till the sea has washed out those words. Paul says, "Madge found strawberries yesterday, and I'm going to look for some now."

"Yes, yes, we do need more flowers," Gran says. "The petals are dropping."

Madge goes for the flower-basket and the secateurs, into the green-and-cream painted kitchen, with its huge windowed dresser, and Amy elbow-deep in dishes in the sink. "That was a super pudding you cooked, Amy," says Madge. "What was it?"

"Queen Mab's pudding, Miss," says Amy. She sounds sulky, thinks Madge, but I would be too if I got left with all the dishes every day. "It's a lovely day, Amy," she says. "Will you have time to go out later on?"

"I've the evening off, Miss Madge, thank you. Walt is coming for me."

"Who's Walt?"

"He's, well, a friend. A soldier off the American base."

Amy is blushing. Madge grins. "Your boyfriend?

28

Oh, have a good time tonight, Amy!" And she goes to join Gran in the rose garden.

"A bowlful of Peace, and one of Rosa Mutabilis, I think," says Gran, sitting on the stone bench at the edge of the rose garden, while Madge cuts the prickly stems and lays them in the basket. They are good children, thinks Gran. They are staying with me now without my asking. Was I as kind at their age? I can't remember . . . she is falling asleep. Seeing her nodding Madge smiles, and goes to cut sweet peas.

The kitchen table is covered with vases, all shapes and sizes, and crumpled chicken-wire, and little lead lumps with spikes on, like heavy hedgehogs. Amy has gone, and the buzz of the Hoover is heard faintly from an upstairs room. Madge fills the silver bowl first, the one with the domed lid full of holes for the stems to go through. That's for the living-room. Then sweet peas – for Gran's dressing-table, and some for me, thinks Madge, for the best spare me that likes sweet peas as much as grown-ups do, and now, I think, these extra roses for Amy's room, because really she has so much washing up to do. Madge goes up and down, carrying the vases upstairs one by one. Amy's room is close, with a heavy smell of scent. A photo of a soldier in American uniform stands beside the mirror on the chest of drawers.

Now, thinks Madge, as she gently stirs the roses in the sitting-room vases to look their best where she has put them, I'll make a cup of tea, and take it to Gran. She comes down the steps to the rose garden, carefully balancing the tin tray with a cup, and a little brown teapot on, and the tinkle of cup on saucer wakes her dozing Gran with a jump. Madge sets the tray down, and pours tea. "How sweet of you, dearie," says Gran, smiling. I was not as kind at their age, she decides. How deeply she wrinkles when she smiles, thinks Madge. I suppose she is still nice to look at because all her wrinkles are on smile lines. Shall I smile enough to grow like that, I wonder? As a start, she smiles now.

"Madge!" Paul calls from the terrace. "Do you want to go fishing?"

"Off you go then, Madge," says Gran at once. "Jeremy asks after Miss Madge and Master Paul all summer, every time we send down to him for mackerel. He'll be glad to see you." Madge runs off, leaving behind her a sense of peace. How good to have them with me, thinks Gran. She has noticed, but is trying not to notice, that really very little of having them with her is enough; they are so bright and restless. She loves them more contentedly when they are not with her, but somewhere off a little way, when she can, without missing them, simply see them in thought. She sips her tea. Madge has forgotten the sugar.

Jeremy's boat, the *Amulet*, is lying at anchor in the harbour, with her faded blue sail furled.

"Why, you've grown again, young Paul," he says. "You'll be after having a boat of your own any day now, and then who'll help with my lines? And Miss Madge here is quite the young lady now I see. Well, well."

"Are you taking the boat out today?" asks Paul.

"Maybe I am," said Jeremy, smiling, "if I can just find someone to see to the lines, while I mind the sail. Wind's pretty." He hands them down into his little rowing-boat, and begins the gentle haul out to mid-harbour, to reach the *Amulet*. Hanging over the side of the boat Madge watches through glassy water the sandy harbour floor falling, falling deeper and deeper, till the height they are floating at goes to her head, and makes her dizzy. Still she can see the rippled sea bottom, and the shoals of little fish swarming half-way down the clear green depth.

The open sea is different. *Amulet* rises and falls, leans in the wind, breasts the slopes of water. Beneath her feet Madge feels the tremulous, living movement of the wood. The wind blows so steady and cool you would think it is a different day from the breathless heat on land. Madge goes to the prow to be showered with beads of spray. Paul opens his chipped blue box, and shows Jeremy his new set of spinners. Jeremy takes the red and silver one in his brown gnarled fingers. "Here's the best one," he says.

"Madge is having that one," says Paul.

Madge is singing, *Speed bonny boat like a bird on the wing, over the sea to Skye!* and over the sea there is sky, she thinks, you can see where they join, and it looks as if you could sail there, and it would be just about as far as Godrevy, for over there Godrevy stands, just on the line where sea meets sky.

"Shall we go round Godrevy?" she asks Jeremy.

"Fish are further in," he tells her, and Paul gives her a line to hold, that trails out behind the boat. "I wish we could come out sailing, and not fish," she says.

"Why, what'd be the point of that?" says Jeremy. So holding her line Madge sits and waits. She looks with distaste at the spinners in Paul's box – little fish

31

made of tin, with hinges and joins in them, so they will spin and flash in the race of water like living things, and for fins and tail they have hooks, sharp little murderous barbed ones. So cruel, thinks Madge, so cruel. I hate to see them die. She feels the jerky tugging begin on her line, and pretends she doesn't.

"Madge, Madge, you've got a bite!" cries Paul, and so she has to haul in her line, while he jumps and cries with joy, for they have sailed over a shoal, and all his lines are dancing. Jeremy puts a loop of rope on the tiller to hold them on course, and helps pull the fishes in.

It takes Jeremy's strong hand to tear the spinners from their throats. He throws them into the cockpit. Gasping for water there, drowning in cruel air, they thump and flap, flailing their strong lithe bodies, beating like trapped birds from one wall to another of the boat. How dark their sea-blue spines! And on their sides dragon markings, electric blue and green, bright and splendid from the water! Blood flies from their exploding gills and spatters round the boat. And when you think they are finished at last, and they lie still on the decking, suddenly they lift their strong tails, and beat – thump – once more. All the while cringing, nearly whimpering with pity and terror, Madge shuts her eyes and winces, and shudders from top to toe as a frantic fish hits into her and slithers down her legs. Spots of blood freckle her legs and arms. When the wild thumping ceases she opens her eyes and then startles and flinches again as the largest fish beats one last dying flap against the floor. Jeremy casually brains it with a wooden pin, while Paul checks the spinners, and runs them over the side again. I suppose girls can't help it, he

32

thinks disgustedly about Madge. I suppose if any girl could, Madge would, he admits to himself, grudgingly. After all, she does like eating them! he adds, exasperated.

Oh I don't mind so much once they are still, thinks Madge, recovering, though she knows well enough that she will mind when it comes to threading string through their gills. Jeremy brings the boat about to sail over the shoal again, and she watches the hazy shore swing round them, and idly tries to pick out Goldengrove, hanging on its perch on the cliff that looks small and insignificant and doesn't tower over the sea at all, from the sea's point of view.

Three times more the death-throes have to be lived through, and then there are fish enough – enough for breakfast at Goldengrove, and enough for Jeremy to sell to landladies on the quay and make it worth his while to have come out. "We must go in now," he says, before Madge has time to ask about sailing round Godrevy. "Weather won't hold."

"*Won't* it?" says Madge, astonished, looking up at the blue, blue sky. But Jeremy points to a black cloud, sun-rimmed, hovering out to sea, and look, thinks Paul, all the other ships are making for harbour now.

So back they go, tacking, leaning in the wind, and mind your heads now! as the boom comes over, back towards home. The harbour stretches out its two stone arms to enfold them, and behind it on the hill the women are taking the sheets in from bleaching, ready to tuck up their men. So, landing, climbing the steep weedy steps to the quay, they go, Paul carrying a stringful of fish, and sending the women who ask him how much, to Jeremy coming just behind him with a boxful.

"Look, Jeremy, what about that boat?" says Paul, pointing at the bay, across which the water has darkened under the spreading cloud, and over which the white horses are beginning to gallop for the shore. For one boat hasn't come in.

"Frenchy," says Jeremy. "Won't be told."

Up the path then, the shining fish fading in the dry air, though still beautiful, swinging against Paul's leg. I'll wash the scales off in the bath tonight, he thinks.

Next morning they come down to mackerel for breakfast. All the roses Madge picked yesterday have unlaced themselves, and are open-heartedly lavishing their scent around the room. The garden is deep in dew, smelling of moisture in heat. The trees of Goldengrove are quietly baking brown. A soft morning haze wreathes the garden.

"A real Indian summer," says Gran.

"Why Indian?" asks Paul, but Gran does not know.

And after breakfast, they go running over the lawn, getting their sandalled toes wet in the grass, and then down the path to the sea. "Look, I brought this to tackle the boat with," says Paul, unwrapping a rusty scraper from his beach towel. It has made a rust mark on the worn white towelling.

"He's not there today!" says Madge, with a lift of the heart.

And neither, she thinks, are those scrawls we

34

made. How clean and entire the sea leaves its beach!

"It's very early. He might come out later," says Paul.

"But he's not there *now*," says Madge. "Come for a swim?" For the sea is very gentle and quiet this morning, and only baby waves are breaking on the shore.

"Too cold just yet," says Paul, but Madge has to find it so with her own toes, and then her knees, before she suddenly decides not to go further, and runs back to Paul. Paul has discarded his shirt, and is busy sharpening his scraper, holding it at an angle against a piece of rock, rubbing it to and fro. Rust powders off it.

"O.K. now," he says, trying the edge gingerly with his finger. Madge looks up, and he says, "He's not there. I just looked."

Then they start to strip off the weed. Madge pulls away great handfuls of black snakes, like the locks of Medusa. Where it is still wet it is very tough, and she borrows Paul's penknife to sever it. He loosens its grip with his scraper, slicing off the suckers where they grip the wood. There are little clusters of tight-fisted barnacles to be shifted too; soon Paul is sweating with the effort, and he wraps his handkerchief round his hand to guard against blistering his palm.

Madge, though, is soon tired of hacking at weed, and carting away prickly handfuls; she soon wants to swap with him. "Let me have a turn with the scraper, Paul," she says.

He gives it to her straight away, though she won't be able to use it, he thinks, and he is quite right, for a red sore place on her hand seems to come almost at once where the round handle of the scraper pushes when you drive it along the surface. So Madge puts the scraper down, and begins to dig sand out of the boat, and the charm of that too fades very fast when she feels how high you have to swing the loaded spade to clear the sides, and toss the sand over and away. Soon she is thinking, surely it is time for a rest, and a swim, and our orange juice, but looking at her watch she finds, astonished, that they have only been working twenty minutes. "I think I'll go and put the orange bottle in a pool," she says to Paul. "To keep it cooler."

"I'll come too," says Paul. For I don't see why I should keep at it longer than her, he thinks. It's her idea to paint it after all.

At the rocky corners of the beach, where the sea covers the stones at high tide, it leaves abandoned pools when it ebbs. Here is one with a sandy floor, and three fishes, very small, catch-and-keep-in-jam-jar-size, and some of the bright green weed, all feathery and leafy-looking, and two sea-anemones, like pustules on the rock. Paul dips a finger in, and gently swirls the water, and it opens groping fronds, looking like a garden pink, and it's really hard to believe, thinks Madge, leaning over the pool to look at it, that it's really searching for meat. But the fishes swerve away from it as they swim.

The bottle of orange stands on the floor of the pool, with only its neck above the surface. "Let's swim now," says Paul.

After swimming they go dripping wet back to the boat. "He's not there yet," says Paul, taking up his scraper again. Perhaps he won't come, he thinks. Madge is thinking, perhaps he won't ever come again.

"Damn!" says Paul sharply. Swift-falling gouts of

36

blood spot the sand in the boat. He claps one hand round another, and blood oozes between his fingers He has gashed himself with the scraper.

"Give me my handkerchief, Madge," he says.

"Oh, it's dirty, Paul, you can't put it round a cut," she says. "Is it deep? Is it bad?"

"It doesn't hurt much, but there seems to be a lot of blood," says Paul. "Do give me that handkerchief."

"No, really Paul, it isn't clean enough. Come on, we'll have to go up to the house for a plaster and some iodine." She wraps his towel round his hand, and leads him away.

As soon as they enter the house, they hear voices coming from the drawing-room. Gran has a visitor; his deep voice is clear and surprising in that house. Madge calls for Amy, and pulls Paul, who is still saying, "What a fuss!" into the kitchen.

They were hoping to creep away to the beach again, with Paul's hand neatly bandaged and cleaned, but looking up from her favourite armchair Gran sees them through the open door, and calls them in.

"Professor Ashton, these are my grandchildren," she says, "Madge and Paul." Sitting opposite her is the blind man. He is holding his head at that un-natural angle, as though he were looking at the join between ceiling and wall.

"Hullo," he says, and smiles, but he does not move his head. His smile is directed over their heads.

"Hullo," says Madge. And I wonder if my father was like this man? she thinks, as she always thinks, meeting any man older than twenty. Of course not, it doesn't seem likely. But how do I know, when

37

everything they tell me is so vague? Even his death, for "Missing in the war" is a very vague way to die.

Gran is saying, "This is Professor Ashton, dears. He is a famous professor of English Literature. And he was a good friend of your grandfather's."

"Hullo," says Paul. He can't think of anything to say.

"So yours are the voices I can hear below me on the beach. Your grandmother has been kind enough to let me take her little cottage for a while," says the Professor. "I won't keep her from you for long. I have just called to pay my respects."

Does he mean pay his rent? wonders Paul. What does one say to him? I'm sure Gran wants us to say something. "It must be rotten to be blind," he offers.

"Paul!" cries Gran, horrified.

But the Professor, tuning in to the direction of Paul's voice, turns his strange, fixed face towards them. Seeing him from near enough, you can see round the huge black pupils of his eyes a tiny rim of blue iris of unchanging width. "Yes, it is," he says. "I find it hard to get used to." Unlike Gran's his voice is not shocked.

"I mean," Paul plunges on, "what do you do all day?"

"I was just going to ask you if you find you can still work, Ralph," Gran breaks in hastily.

"I have some books in braille. But it certainly is difficult to do anything worth while. In London some of my students were kind enough to come and read to me, but down here...."

"I'll come and read to you," says Madge.

The Professor smiles again. "My books would bore you very quickly, Madge, I'm afraid," he says.

"Well, as long as they don't bore you, I'll read

38

them to you," says Madge. "I'll come this afternoon."

"Thank you," he says. "But you mustn't change
your plans for me."

"We weren't planning anything," she says. Bloody
girls! thinks Paul. Well, I'm not sweating on that
boat if she's not. I'm going fishing.

Paul, out in the bay, with the arc of wind-stretched
canvas curving above him, looks at the sleek fish,
jumping and dying at his feet, and thinks of Madge
cringing. He looks shorewards, and sees the white
cottage, framed by golden treetops, and thinks where
she is. Then his line tugs again.

Sitting in a wooden chair in the window bay of
the cottage, draped in sunlight, Madge is reading.
Bright drifts of sea-air float past her, intermittently
wafting across the dusty smell that hangs on the
inside air. Books lie in piles on a dusty table beside
her. Her listener sits in an armchair by the empty
hearth, facing her, with his dog at his feet. You can
stare at him as you never could at anyone else,
Madge finds. His face is crowded, full of events, for
all the blankness of his eyes. Paul's face, by com-
parison, or her own, is empty as the open air. It's not
that he is wrinkled, like Gran; but lines as fine as
spider thread are there; you wouldn't see them unless
you really stared, but they crowd his face with the
ghosts of expressions absent now, with joy and pain.

"Weep me not dead" means: "Do not make me cry myself to death", reads Madge, *"do not kill me with the sight of your tears; do not cry for me as for a man already dead, when, in fact, I am in your arms,"* and, with a different sort of feeling, *"do not exert your power over the sea so as to make it drown me by sympathetic magic; there is a conscious neatness in the ingenuity of the phrasing, perhaps because the same idea is being repeated which brings out the change of tone in this verse.* . . . Her voice is flat and expressionless, and full of tiny unpunctuated hesitations, as she tries to make out what she is reading.

"Are you bored?" the Professor asks her.

"Yes, I mean no, of course not."

"You mean yes. You should say so. You should always say what you think."

"Should I? My mother is always telling me not to."

"No conversation is possible otherwise. You never get to grips with what people are like, if they hide it from you. If people just make polite noises when they talk, then talking's hardly worth the effort."

"You're right, I suppose," says Madge. She is astonished. Talking to grown-ups, she had thought, would always be like one of those trick party-games where you have to try all the time not to make a mistake, and uttering what comes naturally to your lips gets you three black marks at once.

"Now, are you bored?" he is saying.

"Yes – I mean no – I mean yes, I am bored with this horrible book because I don't understand a word of it, but no, I am not bored with being here reading to you, even if the book is horrible."

He smiles. "Nevertheless, let's put the horrible

book away, and read *Alice through the Looking Glass* instead," he says.

"Oh, no, don't let's!" says Madge. "This is the book you need, isn't it? And I didn't come for you to be kind to me, I came to be kind to you!"

"I don't know that I like people being kind to me," he says.

"Whyever not?" she says, astonished again. "I like it lots."

"Well, for lots of reasons, but mainly because they usually stop, sooner or later, just when you have got used to it."

"But I'm not stopping," she says, indignantly, "I'm trying to go on!"

He pauses, then "You go right on then," he says, smiling again. But his smile is very funny, thinks Madge, as she mouths . . . "*What it may doe too soon,*" *since the middle line may as usual go forwards or backwards, may be said of the "sea" or of the "winde"* . . . . It doesn't go anywhere. I suppose it's because his face has no direction, but it's a very inward sort of smile. Like the difference between hugging oneself, and hugging someone else, and his smile hugs himself. And how good I am being, she reflects, as she ploughs on and on through the thicket of words, when I might be out fishing with Paul, or working with him on our boat. I suppose it's my goodness and kindness this afternoon that makes me feel so warm and glowing inside. It must be true that virtue is its own reward. She reads on and on.

"You may stop now," he says in a while. "You need not say you are willing to continue. I have heard all I can take in for today."

"All right." Madge thankfully puts the book down. "But I'm not going yet. I'm going to dust this room before I go home for tea. It's terribly dirty. You should see it!"

"I don't mind what it looks like," he says.

"But it smells of dust!" she protests.

"Really? Does it?"

"That dry tickly smell is dust. Surely you'd like me to get rid of it for you."

"You are being kind again," he says. "But all right, only please don't move anything, or I won't be able to find it."

Madge dusts. She lifts each pile of books in turn, and dusts away the outline of the bottom book on the table, and slaps them together before putting them back. They release a cloud of grey specks when she bangs them against each other. She finds a broom to sweep the floor. The dog growls at it, and she has to sweep round him. The Professor has got out of his chair, and is making tea in the kitchen. Taking the broom back she watches him. The kitchen looks very untidy, but he puts his hand on each thing he needs, just by reaching for it. "You see why things mustn't be moved!" he says. He pours out the tea, feeling first with his left hand for the rim of the cup, to judge where he should pour. But the kitchen is full of scattered tea-leaves, crumbs, small spills and a stale smell, because he can't see his accidents. Madge wipes, and tidies, and picks up the dropped peeled potato that is stinking quietly in a corner by the stove. He shouldn't have to live like this, she thinks. Nobody should, and especially not an important and clever man like him. She sits down and drinks her tea. It tastes funny, a bit like tar smells, but she doesn't like to say so. She gulps it down.

"I must go now," she says, standing up. "But I'll come again."

42

"Thank you very much, Madge," he says, "But you must remember that I don't need kindness."

"Oh, bother kindness!" says Madge crossly. "I shall come to read to you, that is all, Professor Ashton."

"Don't call me Professor," he says.

"Is it wrong? I thought Gran said it."

"I am a professor, but my name is Ralph. I'd rather, if you really are coming again, that you called me that."

"Goodbye, then," says Madge. She was going to say "Goodbye Ralph," but, suddenly embarrassed, she cuts herself short.

Running up to the house she meets Paul, strolling in the garden, with a palmful of tiny strawberries from the grove.

"Done your good deed for the day?" he asks her. "I got enough fish for breakfast all by myself. Look, I think these are the very last of the strawberries, you'd better have some." He counts seven little red heart-shaped seed-studded fruits in his palm. "Three for you," he says, "and four for me, because I found them."

"Could I borrow a mallet from the carpentry box in the shed?" asks Paul, over breakfast.

"What are you doing, dear?" asks Gran.

"You know that boat, down on the beach? Well we're cleaning the weed off it, because we're thinking of painting it."

"You have the mallet, then, by all means," says Gran. "That's a nice little boat. Your grandfather used to go fishing in it." And it hasn't been used for years now, she thinks, except for the children to play in, high and dry on the shore. So long since it floated. When was it, I wonder, when would it have been? I remember my son taking Madge out in it, on a still calm day . . . he sailed all the way to Godrevy, with Madge fallen asleep, I think he said, most of the way, with her head on a coil of rope, and then he had to rest there, and have tea with the lighthouse men. That was before the bitter quarrelling began. . . . Madge was only a child then, a tiny child . . . so long ago . . .

"Good morning Gran," says Madge, with a soap-scented kiss.

"Good morning, dearie. Eat up your fish before Paul fusses to be out and away." But with "See you down there," Paul is off anyway.

"Gran," says Madge, with a mouth full of toast, "I was wondering if I would go again to read to Professor Ashton. Do you think I should?"

"Not if you don't want to, dear. After all you're on holiday here. I'm sure Ralph doesn't expect it."

"But I do want to. And I know he doesn't expect it; he said I wasn't to be kind to him. But I thought, if he's such a clever man, what a waste if he doesn't work. And he could work if he could get the books read to him. I thought I might keep going till I've finished the one he needs now. What do you think, Gran? Is it true one shouldn't be kind to him?"

"Stuff and nonsense, dearie!" says Gran. "One should always be kind to people. If you don't mind going, then it would be very good of you to give him a helping hand. But you won't forget about Paul,

44

dear, will you? You know how he looks forward to playing with you."

"Oh, Paul won't mind," says Madge. "He keeps wanting to go fishing, you know, Gran. And I'm not going till after lunch. I'm going down to the beach with Paul now."

The beach is cooler when they reach it. There is a keen freshness in the wind, though the sea is still mellow with yesterday's warmth. Little puffy clouds scud rapidly overhead, casting patches of shade. Paul shows Madge how to use the mallet; instead of pushing the scraper with your palm, and getting sore, you hold it against the weed and strike it with the mallet, forcing it along the wood. The weed falls off in swathes, and lies like my hair, thinks Madge, when Mummy had it bobbed last year, and great heavy locks fell to the floor round the hairdresser's chair. But the bright green slimy weed is still difficult – the scraper slips on it instead of dislodging it. Madge works very hard, keeping on while Paul goes swimming, trying hard for his approval.

"You don't have to kill yourself over it, Madge," he says, coming back beaded with salt water from his second dip. "There's more time this afternoon."

"I was thinking of going and reading to Ralph this afternoon," says Madge, cautiously.

"But you've done that," Paul says. "You did that yesterday."

"It isn't the sort of thing that stays done," she says. "It's like brushing your teeth; having done it yesterday is no reason for not doing it today."

"But Madge," he wails, dismayed, "you can't mean that! It'll be like fagging for someone, on and on and on."

45

"Not and on and on. Just some each day. I didn't think you'd mind. I thought you'd quite like to go fishing without a cowardly girl along."

And it's quite true, thinks Paul, pulling on his aertex shirt, which sticks on his salty skin, that I'd go out with Jeremy every day if she didn't hate the fish flapping so. But she's crazy, all the same. What is it to do with us, if the man's blind? *She* can't make it all right. . . .

And it's quite true, thinks Madge, that I hate the bloody bit, but I do like the wind and the push, and the rise and fall of it, and I would really rather like to go too. . . . "I was just going to finish what I was reading yesterday," she says.

"Oh, I see," Paul says. "All right. I'll go out with Jeremy."

She goes through the open door, cat-walking, in bare feet. He has drawn his chair into the window recess, to feel the sun, and opened the windows. She has picked a handful of sweet peas in the garden on her way down – "More you pluck 'em, longer they grow," says Mr Arthur. "They keep coming till the frost down here." She goes to find a jam-jar to put them in.

"You did come again," he says, hearing her quiet movements, putting aside his blank-paged, embossed book in braille, and smiling over her head.

"Yes. I said I would," she says, putting the jam-jar on the table, and coming to sit down.

"This book today, please." He runs his fingers over a pile of books, feeling the spines, and picking one out.

"That's a novel," Madge protests. "Can't we read the horrible book again? I do so want to be useful to you!"

"It doesn't have to be a horrible book to be useful," he says, grinning. "Thank heavens! And the book you are rejecting is a masterpiece of literature. Can you start on page 91?"

A woman, reads Madge, *especially if she have the misfortune of knowing anything, should conceal it as well as she can. The advantages of natural folly in a beautiful girl have been already set forth by the capital pen of a sister author; and to her treatment of the subject I will only add, in justice to men, that though, to the larger and more trifling part of the sex, imbecility in females is a great enhancement of their personal charms, there is a portion of them too reasonable –* Ralph was smiling gently – *and too well-informed themselves, to desire anything more in a woman than ignorance.* "Oh!" cries Madge, indignant.

"Go on, go on," he says. "The next bit is delicious."

But Catherine did not know her own advantages; did not know that a good-looking girl with an affectionate heart, and a very ignorant mind, cannot fail of attracting a clever young man, unless circumstances are particularly untoward. In the present instance, she confessed and lamented her want of knowledge; declared that she would give anything in the world to be able to draw; and a lecture on the picturesque immediately followed, in which his instructions were so clear that she soon began to see

47

beauty in everything admired by him; and her atten-
tion was so earnest, that he became perfectly satisfied
of her having a great deal of natural taste. He talked
of fore-grounds, distances, and second distances;
side-screens and perspectives; lights and shades; and
Catherine was so hopeful a scholar, that when they
gained the top of Beechen Cliff, she voluntarily
rejected the whole city of Bath, as unworthy to make
part of a landscape. . . . Madge begins to laugh, and
he laughs too. Like a double wave the two laughters
swell each other, and she can't stop.

"Oh, but listen," she says, when she does get her
breath back, "This isn't work. You just chose this to
amuse me, Ralph, didn't you?"

"Well, it amuses me too," he says. "And I miss
reading for fun quite as much as I miss working.
But your suspicions, Catherine, are quite without
foundation. Go and look at the dark blue file on
the desk."

She wanders over and opens the file. *The novels
of Jane Austen* it says, in typescript. *A critique, by
R. Ashton.* "Oh!" she says, "Can I borrow this?"

"Is it the sort of thing you read?"

"Well, it's the sort of thing on my reading list."

"Yes, you can borrow it," he says.

"Oh, thank you! I've never *seen* a manuscript
before, let alone read one."

"Did you bring me some flowers?" he asks. "Will
you put them within reach?" I couldn't smell them
from across the room, thinks Madge, bringing the
flowers. He's awfully good at that.

He takes the jam-jar, and buries his face in the
flowers. He brushes their multicoloured little butter-
fly wings across his face, to and fro, and draws
breath like a sigh. A gust of their sweetness reaches

Madge, standing beside him, as though his touch had set it free. "They're sweet peas," she says.

"Yes, I can tell," he says, and Oh, how awful of me, thinks Madge, wincing; of course he can. "Shall I read some more?" she asks hastily.

"Do you want to read more?"

"Oh, yes. . . . *"You know what you ought to do* she reads. *Clear your character handsomely before her. Tell her that you think very highly of the understanding of women."*

"Miss Morland, I think very highly of the understanding of all the women in the world, especially of those, whoever they may be, with whom I happen to be in company."

"That is not enough, be more serious."

"Miss Morland, no one can think more highly of the understanding of women than I do. In my opinion, nature has given them so much that they never find it necessary to use more than half . . ." and Oh, thinks Madge, how happy he looks now, smiling all the time at this lovely stuff, and basking in sweet peas. I have made him happy. I read, he laughs. I brought him the flowers. They have done him good. I have done him good. I am happy, reading this, with the sun on the nape of my neck, and the fresh air blowing through the window here, and I hadn't really noticed till now, but when you get used to his eyes, he's really quite handsome, in an aged sort of way. He'd do for Mr Rochester, almost. It's getting late, and I don't want to go. He is Mr Rochester, and I am his Jane. I will come and see him in plain grey alpaca – whatever sort of cloth *was* alpaca? – and call him Sir.

"You've stopped reading, and you haven't moved," he says. "What were you thinking?"

"I was thinking of calling you Sir," says Madge.

"Good grief!" he says, looking really amazed. "Whatever makes you say that?"

"You asking me what I was thinking made me say it."

"I asked for that, in short," he said, smiling.

"I must go now, or I'll be late for tea, and Paul might be cross with me."

"Might he, indeed? You seem very close, for cousins of a different age."

"We have lots in common."

"You both like the beach, you mean?"

"No, I mean we understand each other very well. He has a stepmother, and I have a stepfather, and we know without ever having said anything what we feel about that. You know what I mean; if I didn't see Paul for twenty years, and then I met him suddenly, in the street, I would know at once what sort of mood he was in. I wouldn't have to think about it; I'd just know. There must be somebody like that for you."

"There was once," he says. "But I shall never see her again. Off you go now, or Paul will be cross! And Madge, thank you for coming."

"Gran," says Madge, finding Gran alone in the drawing-room, when Paul has been sent off to bed, slowly putting a green stitch into the chair-seat she is making, "why is Professor Ashton all alone like that? There ought to be someone. You should see his kitchen; it's positively squalid. . . ."

"Oh dear," says Gran, sighing. "I'd better find someone to come in once a week and do round for him."

"No, but, I mean, why hasn't he married some-one?"

"He is – was – married, Madge," says Gran. "It's a sad story. He has had a lot to suffer. First he lost his sight, fighting in the war. When he came home his wife left him. That is why he is alone. I wonder if Mrs Paine has time to spare? She could do with a little extra money I dare say. . . ."

"Oh!" cries Madge. "But how terrible! But his wife – she must be wicked, vile, to be so cruel! How *could* she?"

"Now, Madge, dear, you mustn't talk like that. She was a nice enough woman; I liked her. And it may not have been because he went blind that she left him – we don't know that. Quick to praise and slow to blame – that's the way to be. We never know what another person feels," and best that way, far best not to know, she thinks. This child alarms me.

"But to be left alone. . . ."

"Yes it's hard. Life is hard. That's why I let him have the cottage, though I usually don't like some-one so near. I'm tired of neighbours, and getting on with people. They always want you to make egg-cosies for bazaars or something. . . . But I thought the sea air would do him good. Take him out of him-self a bit."

"Yes of course, but Gran. . . ."

"It's getting late, now, dearie. Late. Off to bed with you. Sleep well."

Coming warm and powdery from the bathroom, and shutting the bedroom door, switching on the little lamp with a rose-spotted china base and scalloped peach-coloured parchment shade that stands beside the bed, she eagerly opens Ralph's manuscript, as though it were a box of chocolates, and props her head on her arm on the pillow to read it, expecting it to prolong the remembered afternoon. But it is all about the Mysteries of Udolpho, whatever those may be, and the metaphysics of irony. How clever he must be, thinks Madge dreamily, I can't understand this at all. But there isn't any laughter in the book, and she is very soon asleep.

Madge sits cross-legged in the sand, working the scraper round the curved boarding of the boat, hacking at weed. Paul comes from the sea to lie on the sand beside her. He looks at the sky. "I suppose you're working so hard because you want to go playing goody again this afternoon."

A cloud falls over Madge's thoughts. "Aren't you going fishing?" she asks.

"Jeremy's going to Newlyn today," says Paul, and oh, hell, he thinks, I'm jolly well not going to *say* I'd like her to stay here with me. He feels angry. She ought to know that.

"I was thinking," Madge lies, for she has only just thought of it, "that it would be nice to walk along the cliffs today. Do you remember the lizards we found last year?"

"Oh yes!" says Paul, and the clouds roll away from him. "And the tails came off in your hand when you tried to catch them. Yes, let's do that, Madge."

"Good, that's fixed then." She goes on working,

making a deliberately long pause. Then, "Paul," she
begins, "if we are going for a walk we could perfectly well ask Ralph to come with us, couldn't
we?"

Oh lord! thinks Paul, Oh hell! He rolls over
abruptly, and watches his hands angrily jabbing into
the sand. The sharp grains driven under his fingernails prick and hurt.

". . . He wouldn't make any difference to us, we
could still go where we like, and catch lizards. He
can't go by himself, in case he falls, he said. His dog
is trained for roads, not cliffs. What do you think,
Paul? Shall we ask him?"

I shall look pretty beastly if I say no, thinks Paul.
Being beastly to the blind – what a part to play! And
why do I mind so, anyway? I haven't got anything
against the geezer, have I? He rolls over again, and
looks up, and sees the Professor sitting blankly, all
alone in his garden. His darkness hangs over Paul
like a cloud. "Oh, all right then," he says. "You can
ask him. I like his dog," he adds, in an attempt to be
nice about it.

The dog, relieved from duty for once, and off the
lead, races and gambols like a puppy on the path
ahead of them. Paul runs and shouts, throwing a
stick for the dog. "What's he called?" he asks Ralph,
wanting to yell the name. "I just call him Dog," says
Ralph. "Or sometimes Hell-hound."

"How foul of you!" says Paul. "Hey, Dog!" he
yells, running after it again.

Madge walks beside Ralph, leading him. She has
to be shown how to do it, since her first thought had
been to put her arm through his. But he needs instead to rest his hand over hers, while she, elbow

bent, keeps her arm steadily pointing in the direction they are going. He can be steered, as with a tiller, that way.

His hand is very heavy and hot over mine, all the time, thinks Madge. I would like to run with Paul. He walks very slowly.

"It is good to stretch my legs again, and be about in the open air," says Ralph. "I used to come here when I was one of your grandfather's pupils. He held reading parties sometimes in the summer."

"It's very nice up here," says Madge. "Always fresh, however hot the day. The grass is very glossy, and there are sea-pinks, and sea-carrot growing," and oh, the view, she thinks, the things you can see from here! The wide sea, filling and frilling the great bight of the bay, and the fishing fleet scattered over the dreaming water – purple shadows in the haze, and the sky so drenched in sunlight that it looks lilac, and the town, and the hill above the town, no sheets pinned out today, and beyond, again beyond, again more sea, and everywhere distances, great distances. Oh, oh, look at me, how far I can see! And I had better not mention anything about it to Ralph. It wouldn't be kind, just as it wouldn't be kind to leave him, and go running after Paul and Dog, and it's an awful pity how being kind doesn't always make you feel warm and glowing, but sometimes, like now, makes you feel hot and cross, and I don't think Paul should have left me with Ralph *and* the picnic box . . . for the wicker handle of the little tea hamper is irking her free hand.

"I like to hear the waves below," Ralph says, and he does hold his head at a silly angle, thinks Madge. Why can't he *pretend* he's looking, so he looks like normal people?

They are nearly at the lizard den, a remembered-from-last-year place with a tumble of rocks and flat stones topping the cliff, with scrubby heather, and gorse growing, and the fleshy-fingered sea-carrot, smelling of school dinner salad, and the tough-stemmed clumps of wiry thrift, and the little butter-yellow bird's-foot-trefoil growing bright against stone and grass. The bees hum loudly here, and the lizards bask and blink on the lichen-blotched sun-baked stones, and then scurry away into dark crevices with a dry scuttering rustle on the stones. Ralph has some difficulty stepping down to the place they want, but with Paul's hand to hold on as well, he manages it. They choose a wide flat stone for him, and as soon as he sits down Madge runs away, breaking free of her hour-long duty, and races, leaping from ledge to ledge, up to the crest of the hilltop behind the stony hollow at the cliff's edge, and then sprinting, forcing her muscles to their utmost possible speed, she careers down the inland slope beyond, wheeling round in a great circle to run half-way up again before collapsing, gasping for breath, in the grass, with a burning feeling in the back of her throat. She lies still for a moment, and then picks herself up, and goes back.

Ralph has got himself propped into a crook of the hillside like an armchair within moments of Madge's flight, and is leaning back in the sun.

"I like that!" says Paul, watching her go.

"She's had enough of my snail's pace, that's all," says Ralph. Dog comes and lies down at his feet, and he nudges the furry flank with his toe. "What does Madge look like, Paul?"

"Oh," says Paul, "she's quite tall. Not thin, not fat. Brown hair, greenish eyes. She has a very absent-minded look most of the time. That what you wanted to know?"

"Some of it," says Ralph. "Is she like her voice, do you think?"

"*I* don't know," says Paul, and what am I supposed to make of a corny question like that? he asks himself. I suppose he means is she pretty, and I know what I think about that, but I'm not telling anyone; I'm certainly not telling *him*. "She's coming back," he says.

Madge sits down and opens the tea-basket. She sets out the bakelite beakers in a carefully balanced row, and pours out the tea, sweet and milky, just how Paul likes it. Then she unfolds the white damask napkin Amy had done up for her, with the ghosts of roses shining in its polished starch, and brings out a pile of cheese scones with blackberry jam. "Yummy!" says Paul, contentedly. He watches Ralph taste his tea, and wince faintly. He grins, and looks out to sea. Calling gulls wheel overhead, and then fly away. The sun feels hot. A droning bee, hanging in mid-air, attempts to share Paul's scone. "Bzzzzz!" says Paul.

"You know, I used to come here as a boy, and then later as a young man," says Ralph. "I can remember this view very well. I can see it in my mind's eye." His voice sounds contented, thinks Madge. What does it matter if he walks slowly and holds his head too high? "Tell us!" she says. "Pretend *we* can't see it, and you have to tell us."

Smiling he says, "Well, starting at the left, you can see the town from here, with the harbour, and the hill called the Island behind the curve of the harbour, with sheets spread out to dry, and then a beach; it has coloured tents for changing in. Behind

56

it is a little green grass – that's the putting green – and behind that the railway runs along a low viaduct, with more houses behind that on a steep rise of the land."

"Oh, yes!" cries Madge, delighted.

"Then the land curves; you can make out, I think, the trees in your grandmother's garden, but not her house. The land curves on, towards us, and you can see back the way we have come. You can see the cliffs, and the promontories of rocks, and the waves breaking over them. And there's nothing else to be seen but the open sea."

"Oh, Ralph," says Madge, "you remember jolly well. You really might be looking at it, for you remember it just as it is!"

"He's forgotten the lighthouse," says Paul.

Madge flinches. But looking, she sees there, undeniably solid and real, the crag of Godrevy, standing out of the swirl of breaking water, with the lighthouse upon it, tall and white, and streaked with salt and weathering. And he, thinks Madge, has lost the lighthouse, for ever and ever, and can never get it back, because he cannot see it, and he cannot remember it, and oh! how much I like it, standing there, not because it is beautiful, but because it is real, and I can see it.

"Lighthouse?" says Ralph. "Oh, yes I seem to recall . . . out to sea somewhere?"

Suddenly Godrevy seems to melt, and waver, like a reflected image in moving water. Madge's eyes have filled with tears.

When she has rubbed them away, she sees Paul's hand crawling over the platform of rock beside him, very quietly, walking on its fingers towards a lizard, a small scaly dragon, that has come out to sun itself.

A little forked scarlet tongue flickers in and out of its crocodile mouth. It is a golden green colour, spotted and mottled.

"Oh no, Paul, don't!" cries Madge, seeing again, in her mind's eye, from last year, the shed tail in Paul's hand, and the truncated creature scurrying away, maimed, and unbalanced, lurching forwards, its broken end bobbing grotesquely upwards as it tried to run without the weight of its tail. Paul makes a grab, and misses. But the lizard, convulsed with fright, breaks in two, and wriggles to safety, leaving its tail behind, anyway.

"Crazy brute!" says Paul, picking up the tail, and looking at it curiously. "I hadn't even touched it!" He thrusts his hand into the crack where the lizard had disappeared, a dark groove running up the rock beside Madge's head, for she is leaning back now, looking idly at the sky.

There is a sudden hiss, like an engine letting off steam. A snake sleeks out of the hot stone, with a silken rustle, and arcs its head, drawn back to strike, beside Madge's cheek.

"Don't move, Madge," says Paul, the colour draining from his face as he sees the black V-marking on the creature's head. It sways, rocking its head to and fro, and "Oh, what is it?" Madge says, and as she speaks it hisses again, louder.

"What is it?" says Ralph.

"Stay still, everyone, and quiet," says Paul, and the tremor in his voice betrays his fright. Oh, bloody stupid snake, it was me who disturbed you, not Madge, he thinks. I shall have to reach out and get you. It would be my legs only, if only you would hit back at me, but it's her face you are aiming for. I must catch you like a lizard, but you won't drop in half and run – you'll twist round swiftly to strike at me, and oh, I'm afraid, he thinks, there ought to be someone to help, there ought to be a grown-up, and thinking of Ralph, just sitting there, looking worried, and what good did that do? he adds, *he's* useless!

Madge lies still. Paul's fright has frightened her, but he doesn't seem to be moving, and she turns her head, very slowly towards whatever it is, till she can see it, narrow, like the bend in a whiplash, and so near she almost screams. From the slope behind her she can hear Ralph's dog, coming back from a foray, beginning to rumble with growl. Oh no, he'll frighten it, she thinks, terrified.

Paul grabs suddenly. He seizes the snake just behind its head, and holds it tight, squirming, in the air. Oh it feels dry! he thinks, not slimy; I'm surprised at its feel. It curls round his wrist, getting a purchase, and with astonishing strength tries to tear free its head. Paul goes to the cliff edge.

"Oh, be careful, Paul, be careful!" cries Madge.

"What is it? What's going on?" says Ralph.

Paul unwinds the viper. He draws it out straight, tail in one hand, head gripped in the other, then he lets it go, with both hands at once, and it falls, twisting and hissing in the air, to the wave-tossed rocks below. "Phew!" says Paul. Running to the cliff edge, Dog barks loudly after the event.

"What is it, What is happening?" says Ralph again.

"It was a viper hissing at me, and Paul threw it over the cliff," says Madge.

Paul looks down at the rocks and waves. He shudders, and rubs his hands on his khaki shorts, trying to get rid of the feel of snake on his palms. I triumph, he thinks, executing a slow, turning war dance on the cliff edge. I am brave, I am swift and sure, I knew what to do, I did not flinch, steady of nerve and hand. I, I, Paul, saved her. I am a knight in armour, I am Perseus with dragons, she owes her life to *me* – it might have killed her, mightn't it? I mean they are very poisonous, I think – how pleased I am, and what use was *he* may I ask?

"It was probably a grass-snake," says Ralph.

"Grass snakes," says Paul, sitting down, and with great deliberation knotting a stem of grass, "don't, I think, have black V-markings on their heads. Grass snakes are a golden colour, and vipers have markings all the way down, and are also rather smaller."

"There. It was a grass snake," says Ralph.

"I am speaking to show you that I am quite well able to tell them apart," says Paul.

Madge thinks, oh, how it hurts me to be able to see the things I can see at the moment. I know why Ralph doesn't want to believe it – he doesn't like to think he was just sitting there while danger threatened that was averted by someone else. And I know why Paul is so pleased with himself; it is because he did it, while a grown-up sat by and did nothing. I wish I did not see. I liked it better when people were like rocks or waves to me; they did what they did, and I understood nothing about it.

"But did it bite you, Madge?" says Ralph, suddenly urgent. "I mean, if it was really a viper we have to cut the wound, cut it deeply, and suck the venom out."

Madge's fingers fly swiftly to touch her smooth cheek, where it curves over her cheekbone at the point the snake had threatened. Pain, blood and a scar! she thinks.

"It *was* a viper," she says firmly, thanking Paul

60

with all the looking she can do. "But it didn't bite me. Paul threw it over the cliff."

"Good for Paul, then," says Ralph, "whether it was a viper or not."

Paul makes a face at him, and thumbs his nose. And Madge, instead of frowning, as he really expects, grins. For a long moment they exchange conspiratorial smiles under Ralph's unseeing eyes. Then, leaning towards each other they mouth soundlessly, in unison, the words IT WAS A VIPER.

"Perhaps we had better start back," says Ralph, "since I take so long over this rough ground."

Hopping along behind as they go, Paul mimics Ralph. He looks – head in air – not where he is going, and puts his feet down tentatively, and stumbles a little, and makes joyful faces. A great affection for Madge fills him. You soppy goose, Madge, he tells himself, grinning. But Madge, with Ralph's arm over hers again, feeling his every step, in forced sympathy with his difficult walking, soon finds Paul unkind – though unseen he does no harm – and frowns him off. In a little while Paul comes and takes Ralph's other arm, and helps her help him home.

"Thank you very much for a delightful afternoon," says Ralph at his door.

Alone in the best spare room, which is filled with soft evening light, Madge wonders what it is like to be blind. She looks out of the window, and sees that the trees are now golden, rust and beautiful. They must turn earlier down here, she thinks, for surely everything was green at home still. Perhaps home is changing while I'm here. If I were blind all seasons would be the same. No, they wouldn't. They each have their own smells. You can feel mist as well as see it. You can hear leaves underfoot when they have fallen. Only sight has gone. I wonder what it's like.

She closes her eyes tightly, and begins, hands outstretched in front of her, to move across the room. About three paces, she thinks, and then I'll reach the bed. She takes three, four, steps forward, and gropes for it. It isn't there. She opens her eyes, and finds herself facing in the wrong direction. She has missed the bed by yards. Oh, but looking is cheating, she tells herself. I must keep my eyes quite shut. She begins again, moving towards the bed. Something under foot. She probes with her toes, wriggling them in her sock. My shoes, she thinks, pushing them away with her foot. It's really quite easy: you have to know what's in the room; that's why he asked me not to move anything. There is a sharp pain on her shin, and she trips up, and falls headlong. She finds herself sitting on the floor, eyes wide open, looking at the dressing-table stool, over which she has fallen. Oh, I mustn't open my eyes, she scolds herself. That's no good, that's not what it's like at all. I would have to find out by feeling what it was I had tripped on. She rubs her shin furiously, gets up, closes her eyes, and begins again.

She crosses the room, and is on her way back before she trips again. And as soon as she stumbles she finds her eyes open again. She hasn't looked down to see what it was, but the moment the unknown something tangles her feet her eyelids spring apart, and she finds herself looking at the opposite wall. "Oh damn!" she cries. It's my dress that tripped me, of course. I just dropped it on the floor as usual. A punishment for slovenly habits – gosh, I bet you have to be fiendishly tidy if you're blind, and you can't even see where you are putting things! I am going to start again. I am going to do something with my eyes shut, instead of just blundering around. She moves towards the little wooden stand on which her towels hang. I shall get my things, and go and wash without looking, she decides. First my towel. She goes towards it, hands outstretched, until she finds herself touching the wall. I'm facing the wrong way again, she thinks, and at the thought her eyes flutter, and a little grey light, filtered through her lashes, gets in. She shuts it out again at once, but it has already leaked to her what is wrong with the towel-hunt: she hasn't come in the wrong direction, but is groping too high. She reaches down, and takes the towel. Now for my sponge-bag, she thinks. Where did I leave it? Hanging on the brass bedpost at the foot of the bed. She rotates, and begins towards the bed again. She finds the bedpost, cool, shiny-smooth in her hands, but the sponge-bag isn't there. I wonder if I hung it on the other one? she thinks, and at once claps her hand to her eyes to stop them cheating her. She gropes for the other bedpost. An image of the bag she is seeking fills her mind; it is made of green rubber-backed canvas with a drawstring through the top, and a little worn Cashe's tape saying *M. FIELDING* sewn in a loop round the string. But the look of it's no good, she knows; it's the feel of it I need to find it by. Her hands run up and down the second bedpost, from the round, palm-filling knob on the top to the place where the soft swelling of the bedclothes presses against it. No bag. Madge sits down, and presses her fists into her disobedient eyes while she tries to remember where she has put the beastly thing. Her eyelids are fighting her now, fluttering upwards, and when she grits her will and defeats them they let through not light, but the feel of light, telling her with a colourless brightness which way the window is. She feels herself tugged by the light as though she were a moth, hating to face away from it, empty and useless though it is. But I didn't know till now that eyelids, aren't solid, like black-out, thinks Madge, punishing them with the pressure of her knuckles.

Suddenly she smells it. The bag is quite near. The smell of rubber and old soap that it emits has come clearly to her nose. She understands at once what has happened – the weight of the bag has pulled it down past the mattress and blankets, and it is hanging lower than she has been feeling for it. Triumphantly she reaches out and gets it. She jumps up, and recklessly speeds towards the door, so that it smacks her face just as she is reaching out a hand for the doorknob. Out onto the landing, across and a little to the left – would it be about three paces? – to the bathroom door. But on the second pace she bumps into something. Better-disciplined at last, she stands still, eyes tight shut, and tries to feel over whatever it is, instead of looking. It is large, and warm, with a knitted surface. It is Paul.

"Whyever can't you look where you're going, Madge?" he yells. "And what the hell are you doing standing there with your eyes shut and that dopey look on your face, waving your hands?"

64

Madge opens her eyes, and blushes. Paul is standing on one leg, rubbing the toe she has trodden on. That's why he's cross, I hurt him, she thinks. "I was trying to see what it would be like," she admits, shamefaced.

"You can't do it like that," says Paul. "You keep opening your eyes. It doesn't work."

"I know," she says. "It isn't working."

"You need a blindfold," says Paul. "Hold on, I've got just the thing." He hurtles away up the attic stairs, taking them two at a time. He comes back quickly, holding something behind his back. "Turn round, and I'll tie you up," he says.

Whatever it is he has put round her eyes feels silky; his school scarf perhaps. He ties it very tightly with a firm hand. "Hold on," he says. "That's not good enough yet. You can always see a bit squinting downwards, where your nose pushes it away from your cheeks." He stuffs something underneath the blindfold, little pads of something, smelling faintly of mothballs, tucked in either side of her nose. "There you are," he says, "that should do it." He sits down on the stairs to watch Madge negotiate the landing. It's not like closing your eyes, because you always open them a bit, he is thinking, and it's not really like being blindfolded either, because you know you can always take the blindfold off. I know what, I'll fix that for her, too!

Safe from cheating, enfolded in her black silk, Madge explores the bathroom. She finds at once that she can't wash her teeth – there's no way of telling her toothbrush from Paul's just by the feel. Gran's on the other hand is easy: its bristles are splayed out sideways in a flattened tangle. She ought to get a new one, thinks Madge. Somehow the game is easier with the blindfold on. She can concentrate on finding her way instead of spending half her energy on her eyelids. She returns to the landing, confident now, needing only a swift touch on the door-frame to find her way. She is almost enjoying the soft darkness; it has a melted feeling to it, all distances dissolved, near and far, everything reduced to what you can feel.

Paul's voice says, "See if you can find your way to my room." Then she hears his steps, going up ahead of her. She reaches out for the bannister-rail, and sliding her fingers up it, slowly climbs the stairs. At the top she takes a big step, as though there were an invisible extra stair, and stumbles. She goes along the narrow landing, trailing a hand on either wall, and reaches for the door. Paul's voice, very close to her, and somehow tight and cold says, "No, you've got the wrong one. To your right."

"You mustn't tell me," she says.

"All right, I won't," says Paul, but now her hand is on the doorknob, and she goes in. But I've got it wrong again, she thinks, for I was sure I needed to go further for Paul's door. His room feels hot and heavy, and smells of dust. Amy can't have been up here all week! thinks Madge. Funny. She moves to where the bed is, the one that used to be hers, and sits down on it. It seems to be covered with things – she feels over them – in cardboard boxes. Whatever had he been collecting? she wonders. "Paul?" she says, but she knows before she says it that he has gone, or rather that he did not enter the room with her. It is not only that she has not heard him, but something else – the feel of him is not here. And funny she thinks, that people have feels around them, like magnetic feels, magnetic *fields* I mean,

and you don't notice when you can see them, because you think it's the sight of them that you feel,
when all the while it is this other thing, like a ghost,
and that of course, is how Ralph knew there was
somebody, and kept saying "Who's there?" the day
we ambushed him. And I'm tired of this now. It
feels so hot and heavy and hard to breathe – it really
does smell dusty in here, and as though no window
has been opened for weeks – and the darkness is
choking me.

She reaches up and tries to untie the blindfold.
Paul has tied it very tightly in a double knot, and she
cannot undo it. She gets up and goes towards the
door, to find Paul to help her. She falls over something at once, and, groping around on hands and
knees where she has fallen, her hands find other
things too, funny things, whose shape she cannot
fathom. The door is beyond the end of Paul's bed,
she thinks, so if I find that – but she can't find that –
it seems not to be there, and oh, what *are* all these
things she is falling over? She remembers her dress,
and the dressing-table stool, and the mysteriousness
of them when they tripped her. But even so she is
beginning to feel scared, blundering and tripping
around in the bright uncluttered attic room that
seems suddenly full of strange bulks and lurking
shin-breakers, crowding in on her, lying in wait with
malice. I must see! and with a sudden lurch of panic,
painfully tweaking the strands of hair that are
knotted into the scarf, she tears off the blindfold.

It is still dark!

Of course, she says to herself, a flash of terror
dying out in relief, I forgot to take off those pads
Paul put beneath it! Her fingers go to her eyes, and
find nothing but naked lids and lashes. A knot of

something, like a swallow down a dry throat, presses on her neck and chest. She feels as though the floor were falling, like the first downward plummet of a descending lift. She can't see. Her mind will not accept the darkness as distance without light – instead it seems a solid thing, a something, like the blindfold, a thick curtain, a cloud, that wraps her, and closes her in, and cuts her off from light that lies beyond. She strikes out blindly, and begins to run, falling over, and leaping up, and crashing into something else, and screaming with fear.

On the landing Paul stands between the open door of his room, in which the clear evening shines, reflecting brightness off the view of the sea, and the usually-locked door of the lumber room, through which he has misguided Madge. He waits and waits and then he hears Madge scream. Well, she wanted to *know*! he tells himself. But he is taken aback by the horror-film note in her scream. From below in the house he hears Gran calling, "What's the matter? Oh, whatever is happening?" He hears her labouring up the stairs, and Amy's running feet coming too, much faster. Hell! Hell to pay, he thinks.

Madge's screaming dies away in sobs. She stands stock still, wide-eyed, staring, and the darkness flows into her, and overwhelms her, like water in death by drowning. A grey line divides the wall of blackness. A vague, furry line, like a chalk mark on a blackboard. Her eyes cease swimming, and narrow to a focus on it so abruptly she can feel them doing it. She is looking at light leaking through a crack. Like a great receding wave the darkness draws back out of her, and belongs to its true place, in the room around her. She is in a dark room, with light leaking round the door. The lumber room, of course! She reaches out a hand for the door catch, and opens it.

Gran and Amy reach the top of the stairs, Gran red-faced, panting for breath. Madge opens the door, and appears, blinking, white as a ghost, with a strained and tear-marked face.

"What is going on?" asks Gran.

"It's my fault, Gran," says Paul. "I locked Madge in the lumber room."

"Whatever has come over you, Paul?" says Gran, and her voice is angry, so that with a small surprise Paul thinks, she can be like other grown-ups if one has been bad enough. "That's not like you. That kind of trick is neither clever nor funny, just unkind. You will go to bed now, without supper."

"Yes, Gran," says Paul, feeling at once how hungry he is. And it's not fair! he tells himself sitting in the attic window, looking at the sea, I wasn't playing tricks. She wanted to *know*, didn't she?

Downstairs Madge eats small bites from her loaded plate. Her napkin, spread out on her lap is ready for anything she can slip onto it. The buttered roll that went with soup, for instance, and one small slice of her roast pork, to put into it, and the fluffy meringue from the dessert. She is ashamed of having screamed loudly enough to have got Paul into trouble, and her heart aches for him, upstairs, alone and hungry.

I only did it for her, and she's downstairs pigging herself, thinks Paul. Bloody girls! But he knows he had not meant it kindly.

In a while there is a tap on the door, and Madge's voice saying, "Paul". She comes in with her napkin-ful of loot, and spreads it out in front of him. She

69

had the impression that she was sacrificing all the nicest bits of her own meal, but it looks rather woe-begone and tatty now, and she says apologetically, "This was all I could get, I'm afraid."

"Better than nothing," he says, tucking in. When he has mouth-room for words he says, "Madge was it really scary?"

"Horrible!" she says, shuddering. "Worse than anything. If it had really gone, I would have done anything, given up anything, to get it back."

"I read a story about that once," says Paul, licking a scoop of pink tongue round his meringue, in a long pause. "The Valley of the Blind, and this man gets into it over the mountains. And he thinks he will lord it over them, and be king, because he can see. But they just think he's seeing things – you know, they think he's mad, and their doctors say that the two round swellings in his head are pressing on his brain, and giving him illusions, and he'll be all right if they operate, and take them out. And he wants awfully to stay, because he's gone soppy about this blind girl, and he wants to marry her, but just the same, when it comes to it, he funks it, and starts to climb out of the valley, even though he knows he won't possibly make it."

"Ugh!" says Madge. "Yes, I bet he would, though. He'd just have to."

"Well, when we had to read it last year in class, I didn't really believe it," says Paul. "I thought he'd have taken what he could get, and done without eyes, just to stay alive. But you know, Madge, you did scream most terribly *awfully*."

"It was terribly awful," says Madge, and her face goes suddenly sad as she thinks, no grey lines appear, and no doors open ever, to let *him* out!

"Hey, listen, someone's coming," says Paul. Madge gets up and opens the door to listen. Someone is coming slowly upstairs. Madge slithers through Paul's door, and scurries down to her bedroom, closing the door on herself there just as the footsteps reach the main landing. They go on past her, up to Paul. Whew! she thinks, thank goodness I made it. It's bad enough having anger and punishments at Goldengrove, anyway, but if I'm caught breaking the quarantine it will go on and on, instead of stopping at this.

There is a tap at Paul's door, and Gran comes in. She is carrying a tray, which she puts on the bed. "You are a very bad boy, Paul dear," she says, and she still sounds upset, "but I can't really let you go hungry. Now eat this, and then go to sleep. Goodnight."

Paul lifts the cloth off the tray. He expects to find bread and water, but Gran has relented further than that; there is a cold pork and chutney sandwich – he can see from the rough cut of the bread that Gran has made it herself, for Amy cuts neater squares – and a little bowl of raspberry jelly with meringue. I bet I'd have got only one meringue if I'd have been having proper supper, thinks Paul, grinning.

Later, when he is already sleeping, a tap on the door disturbs him. Amy comes in, with her best coat and hat still on, and a little paper bag in her hand. "Wake up a mo, Paul," she says. "I've brought you something. Your gran's quite right, mind, but she hardly eats a thing herself these days, she's forgotten what a growing lad needs. I brought you this, look."

She gives him a little bag of hot chips, and a small bar of chocolate, American chocolate, Paul notices, so it has come from Walt. "Oh, thanks, Amy," says

Paul, trying to sound as if he means it, and already wondering where to get rid of the chips, so that Amy won't find them when she clears up next day. But when Amy has gone Paul finds that he has in fact plenty of room for the chips, and more than half the chocolate too.

"You pig! You absolute *hog!*" says Madge when he tells her about it. "And to think I gave you my meringue!"

That morning Madge, getting up, puts on a white organdy dress, one that her mother bought her for going out in. Amy has found it stuffed and crumpled into the dressing-table drawer, rescued it and pressed it and hung it up in the wardrobe, as if she hadn't better things to do, Madge has thought, for I shan't wear it, and it will get crushed again in the suitcase going home. But now she is wearing it, and looking into the mirror to see why her mother likes it. She looks fresh and crisp in it; a high round collar gives her a controlled look, and its soft, see-through-to-the-lining, tissue-paper material looks misty and dreamlike. Madge notices with astonishment how her image flirts with her eyes, has the smug, guess-what look, the something-beautifully-wrapped look of a birthday present. Doesn't go much with matted hair, she thinks, seizing a brush to torment herself into smoothness. And why does Mummy like it? It isn't at all the sort of thing *she* wears. Never mind, I like it too. And I want to feel nice today. I want to be good to be with. It's the least one can do for him,

72

poor him, locked in the lumber room for ever! Oh, how terrible. And oh, *hell*! what with all this dressing I've forgotten to wash! She gets out of the dress again, struggling with the tiny translucent buttons, and grabbing towel and sponge-bag, runs for the bathroom.

Seeing her come down late for breakfast, chocolate-box-pretty, and very careful how she sits down in her chair, Paul scowls. Not even the morning for me, he thinks.

And oh, it's beginning again, thinks Gran, I see it beginning again. Only a dress this morning, at first only dresses and smiles, and then will come longing and yearning, and wanting too much of someone, and raging, raging, against what cannot be. It is always the same. Where does it come from, all this? All over long since for me, now, and not yet begun upon for them, and in between, such storms! She remembers the storms, not wanting to, so that her mind skitters rapidly through years like moments – her son marrying, and the children being born, and the misery she never understood, for why couldn't they resign, accept, and what was the use of either her son or her daughter-in-law complaining to her, accusing each other? I didn't want to hear, thinks Gran, I didn't want to know. And in the end, when they each went their own way, quarrelling about the house, the books, and whose is the grandfather clock, and whose are the children, and dividing them, like so much furniture, Madge with her mother, and Paul with his father, for "I must and will have the rearing of my own son", and, but for me, they would never meet again . . . shocking, shocking. She hears her son saying, "Paul's all right

73

– better with his new mother." She hears her daughter-in-law saying, "Madge doesn't miss her father – not in the least. She can't even remember him." And it never occurs to either that the children might need each other, she grieves, brother and sister, they belong together, together, see how happy we all are together at Goldengrove. Old I may be, but I'm cunning, cunning enough for them. I'll pretend all that stuff and nonsense about cousins if pretend it I must – do they *realise* it makes my one son two, and I have to keep on and on, lying and inventing whenever the subject comes up, and oh, what a tangled web we weave – but as long as death spares me, I'll bring the children together here, and heal the breach, and right the wrong. . . .

"Oh Gran, *please* can you pass the butter?" says Madge, obviously for the third time of asking, and startles her Gran back to her here-and-now granddaughter, crisp in white organdy, wanting butter on it, and, Gran thinks, oh, it's beginning again. . . .

"You look pretty this morning, dearie," she says.

"She doesn't, she looks wet," says Paul. "People don't wear that kind of dress for the morning."

"Well, I've only got one best dress," says Madge unshakeably pleased with herself, "so it must be all right for any time. I've never heard of having three different bests for morning, afternoon and evening." Though Jenny Martin did say she had two, she thinks.

Not even the morning for me, thinks Paul, but it's my fault, I suppose, for I made her feel like this, when I made the Valley of the Blind in the lumber room. . . . There might be conkers in the grove this morning, with the wind last night, and there's sure to be Jeremy fishing, and the sand and waves and

74

the shining light on the shore, but I'd better be nice about it all, to make up for last night, and "I think I'll come with you, if you're going to read this morning, Madge," he says.

Oh *lord*! thinks Madge, dismayed, the shine going off her morning at once, he *would*! "You don't have to, Paul," she says, "if you'd rather be on the beach."

"No, I want to come," he says, lying, for her face has betrayed her.

"We read awfully difficult books, you see," she says. "You won't understand a word."

"That's all right," he says, grimly. "I won't mind that." The more I don't want him to come, the more he will come, sees Madge, resigning herself.

"Have we time to look for conkers?" asks Paul, as they go down through the garden.

"Oh, yes, I expect so," says Madge, but there are none to be found, though the tender green spiky globes can be seen all over the tree. It is tight-fistedly hanging on to them. There is a mist in the air; the day is suspended, uncertain whether it promises a chill, or a hazy heat. The weather is wearing organdy too, thinks Madge.

"How good of you to come, how good of both of you," says Ralph. "I was just wondering how to pass the time. I would like some poetry; I almost need it. Will you mind reading poems?"

"No," says Madge.

"Not as long as they're not about daffodils," says Paul.

"I want one particular thing," says Ralph, "and daffodils don't come into it. Can you find the Milton, Madge? Will you read from *Paradise Lost* – the beginning of Book Three?"

75

Hail, holy Light, offspring of Heav'n first-born,
Or of th' Eternal Coeternal beam
May I express thee unblamed? . . . reads Madge.

And settling to listen, Ralph turns towards Madge, towards the window, and leans back into his chair. Paul sits on the floor, and traces patterns in the dust on the unswept boards. She reads, he listens, and this leaves me out, he thinks. And she was quite right, I don't understand a word of it. Not a word. But it reminds me . . . what of? he wonders, as the words roll on and on. . . . He wonders till he remembers being taken to Winchester by his father, one winter's afternoon, and when they heaved open the slow and heavy door, and stepped inside, the gloomy, unlit, stone-cold space was full of organ music. He remembers the sound now; it was huge and grand, but jumbled somehow in the echoing arches and fluted vaults, so that he could not make out the tune. Now Madge's voice, gone solemn, as in church, rolls out a magnificence in which he cannot find the sense.

. . . Thee I revisit safe, she reads,
And feel thy sovran vital Lamp; but thou
Revisit'st not these eyes, that rowle in vain
To find thy piercing ray, and find no dawn . . .

and something has gone wrong with Madge's voice, which is shaking and trembly, and the music stumbles. *So thick a drop serene hath quenched their Orbs,* she quavers, helpless, as the tears get into her throat, and she cannot see the lines, and sniffs desperately, and says, "Oh, Ralph, surely you don't want *this!*"

"What's wrong? What's the matter?" says Ralph.

with the peaceful and absorbed expression fading from his face. "But I do want it. Won't you read on?"

"I can't," she says, tears flowing freely. "Ralph, how *can* you?"

"Oh, give it here, Madge, do!" says Paul, very cross, grabbing the book from her, "I *can*!" And of course it's what he wants, he thinks, he wants to wallow in it, as he looks for the line. Then in his best, reading-the-lesson-in-the-morning-assembly voice, he goes steadily on.

> . . . *Seasons return; but not to mee returns*
> *Day, or the sweet approach of Ev'n or Morn.*
> *Or sight of vernal bloom, or Summer's Rose,*
> *Or flocks, or herds, or human face divine;*
> *But cloud instead, and ever-during dark*
> *Surrounds me . . .*

His clear, cold voice is interrupted by Madge, sobbing.

"Thank you, Paul, leave it," says Ralph.

"Yes," says Paul, "I will. I'm going down to the beach. Right away!"

He leaves a long silence behind him, in which Madge, wiping her hot cheeks with the flat of her hands, wishes that she were the sort of person who remembers to have a handkerchief.

"What upset you?" says Ralph at last.

"That did."

"Why? Why should it?"

"Oh, but how can you bear it? How can you bear to rub salt in your wounds like that?"

"Rub salt? It doesn't rub salt, it helps. It objectifies."

"I don't understand," says Madge, leaving off

77

wiping her cheeks, as the tears at last dry up. Her hands are sticky with salt like the sea.

"No, indeed you don't," says Ralph, dryly. "But then, why should you, after all?"

"Oh, but I want to, I really want to! What does 'objectify' mean?"

"It means it puts things outside me. Makes them into objects, external to the mind."

"I understand that," says Madge, confidently, for she is remembering the crack of light round yesterday's door, and how it made the darkness flow out of her terrified mind, and become instead just darkness in the room around her, "but I don't understand how it does it."

"Another man's pain, against which to measure one's own. A scream to put against one's own silence. It helps me to grasp how much of what I am is blindness, and how much is me . . . really, this is ridiculous. I never talk like this. It fails. Don't worry your head about it. Change the subject."

Madge suddenly feels like going and putting her arms round him for comfort. She is remembering running to someone with a cut knee, long ago, sometime long ago, arms outstretched, needing the hug to comfort herself. It is an insubstantial sort of wanting, a thin ghostly sort, that fades swiftly in the reality of standing in a dusty room, looking at a dignified middle-aged face, with the eyes stretched open eternally.

"I can't help worrying my head about it," she says.

"My dear Madge," says Ralph, getting up, and groping his way to the window, standing there not-looking out, back turned on her, "I don't want your worry. I don't want your kindness. I am well able to look after myself. I don't want your tears. They spoil your reading voice. And I did want your reading voice."

"Oh, I'm sorry, Ralph, truly I am!" she cries, seizing the book from the table where Paul tossed it as he left. "I'll begin again, and I'll do it properly this time."

"No," he says. "Another day, another book will do. Leave it now. Go with Paul; go and play."

"Can I come back this afternoon?"

"I am going out this afternoon."

"Tomorrow?"

"You can if you want to. I am not asking you to."

"No," she says, "no. All right. Goodbye then."

Leaving, she walks out into open air that is blue with distance. She sees the harbour, and the grey, beige, yellow, tiled and lichen clad houses of the town, and behind them over the roofs the sea again, and she takes the path going down, over the little bridge over the railway, onto the grassy and flowery cliff, and down to the beach and Paul, where the water rolls and piles up layer upon layer, and shines and jumps and breaks and booms on the resounding stretched yellow drum of the shore. Paul looks up smiling, pleased to see her, thinking she has come because of him, and hands her a scraper and she joins in attacking the boat.

"Ugh!" he says. "It's jolly stuffy up there. And if we keep at this till lunch we'll have all the weed off, and we can begin to paint."

This is the ninth day, thinks Paul, picking up his chop by the bone and hoping Gran won't notice. But we didn't start the boat till the second day. It's taken eight days, and there are three days left to go. If we painted it this afternoon, it would be dry by tomorrow – wouldn't it? How long does paint take to dry? I think it would. There would be tomorrow and two more days to play in it. It will be super fun, he tells himself, doubtfully. For he is rather vague about what exactly they will do with it when it is painted and finished. Madge wanted it painted, he reflects. She will think of a game for it. There would have been a lot more days for games if she had helped me more with the work. How many times has she helped on it? Not more than three or four. She isn't such fun as she used to be.

"Paul, dear, what a way to eat a chop!" says Gran mildly.

"Cave man!" says Madge, grinning. But I like her just as much, he tells himself, suppressing his disloyal thought, and another thought adds painfully – or more.

I promised Higgy I'd read while I was down here, Madge is thinking. It's funny, I always think I'll have masses and masses of time when I'm down here, and then there doesn't seem to be a single moment to spare, and the time goes by so fast, I can't bear to count how little must be left. In a way I *have* been reading. We have read nearly all the way through the horrible ambiguity book, hours and hours of it, and *Northanger Abbey*, and quite a lot of *Through the Looking Glass*, and we wasted this morning on Milton. She colours slightly as she thinks of it.

The fresh sea air puts roses in their cheeks, thinks

Gran, contentedly. They come and go in my house. Soon they will be gone. I shall miss them. I shall go to sleep after lunch, and to bed earlier in the evening. I shall think about them, and buy postcards to send to them at home. Then they will return. They will come back every year. Like the swallows, like the storms.

After lunch they go running down the hill into the town, with holiday money clenched in fists in pockets, hot, and smelling metallic and promising chocolate as well as paint. Through narrow streets they go, to the quay, where gulls and shoppers drift along the waterfront from window to window, and a row of boats lies high and dry along the quay beside the railing, ready to ride out the winter earthbound. Laity's shop is there, opposite the green harbour water which slops and rocks, and cradles the anchored boats. Stopping, they peer in, past the rows of stem ginger pots, tied up with straw, past the blackboard with the prices of different kinds of tea chalked up on it like a cricket score, to stare at the rows of green tins, faded with time, on which the battered white clipper ships lean and race across painted panels. "Can I help you, young lady?" says a voice within the shop.

"I was just liking your tins," says Madge. "But perhaps Gran would like some of your tea."

"We try to be different," he says. "Your grandmother drinks Orange Pekoe. Half a pound?"

Then, clutching the dark green and shiny gold packet with a dragon and a crunchy feel, Madge returns to Paul, outside, and they go on towards the fishermen's Co-operative. That, too, has a fine window, full of copper ships-lights, and brass bells, and waxed twine on spools for fishing lines, and boxes of spinners, and dark green glass balls to float the fishermen's nets. They go into the shop, brushing past hanging oilskin jackets and sou'westers, and find themselves in cavern-like gloom. The roof is covered with stalactites made of pendant clusters of sea-boots and fishing rods; all around them rise stalagmites of piled-up socks and sweaters, and bales of netting, and new lobster pots. They consider the colour card for paint, with little sun-faced squares to choose from.

"Which colour is sky-blue-pink?" asks Paul, and pointing at bright sea-green, Madge says, "That one."

"I'll order it for you," says the man behind the counter.

"Oh, haven't you got them?" says Paul, disappointment showing all over him. "We wanted to do it this afternoon."

"Too many of 'em," says the man. "We can't keep them all. But it only takes a day or two to get them. You'll have to have patience. Unless you'd like to use something I have got."

"Well, what have you got?" asks Madge.

"Black and white, of course, and a few oddments. Plenty of cream – lots of people like that. And Lincoln green. And chocolate brown. That's all. How about green and cream?"

"Ugh!" says Madge.

"Just like school corridors," says Paul.

"It's not even the right sort of green," says Madge.

"It's an 'orrible sort of green, I grant," says the man. "Funny you wanting that other colour, for I have got some of that put by, though I can't let you have it. We had it ordered for a Frenchy, said he'd come for it next time he was this way. That was last year, and he's never been back. Can't heed a word they say, that lot. They lie like flatfish!"

"Perhaps he wasn't telling lies," says Paul. "Perhaps he's been shipwrecked, and drowned, and he doesn't like to collect his paint in case you're unkind to ghosts!"

"What's that?" says the man. "Here, don't you go joking about shipwreck round here, young man, because 't'aint funny. Be off with you!"

Outside the shop, resigned to waiting for the paint, they stand undecided.

"I say, Madge," says Paul, his eyes drifting over the harbour to Smeaton's Quay, festooned and cobwebbed as usual with nets hung out to dry, where he can see Jeremy, at the foot of the steps, putting tackle in his dinghy, "If we can't put the paint on today, anyway, might it be a good day to go fishing?"

"Well," says Madge, closing her eyes against the image of wild fish, flapping blood, "yes, why not? Except, would you mind awfully, Paul, if I didn't?"

"Would you mind awfully being left on your own?"

"No, not a bit. Catch a big fish for me, I'm ravenous in the morning. And you could use your red spinner yourself, then."

"Great, see you later," says Paul, beginning to run. Madge watches him go. She wanders over to lean on the harbour rail, and sees the shoals of little fishes swarming in the water, and the wavy sand on the bottom. The foot of the harbour wall has a fringe of submerged weed that waves in the moving water like hair in a slow-motion wind. Soon she can see Paul, very little and far away, climbing into Jeremy's dinghy. She sees the dinghy pull out to the *Amulet*, sees the sail flapping, running up the mast, sees Paul casting off from the big rusty buoy, and watches the *Amulet* tilt on the wind and sail out into the bay.

Now I am alone, she thinks, what shall I do? And for a while she does nothing, but simply stays where she is. Then, I'll climb the Island, she thinks, and sets off up a steep crooked cobbled lane to reach it. Up the green slope she climbs, and gains the little chapel on top. It has a stone cross at each end of its roof, and a little low wall like a gunwale all round it, and it looks like Noah's ark, grounded. An old man in a dark blue sweater is leaning on the wall, looking seawards, smoking a pipe. Madge looks too, at the white horses dancing all over the dark blue bay as far as Godrevy, at the lines of great surf rolling onto the beach beyond the Island, that faces ocean, not bay.

"It's windy today," she says.

"Ay, but there's no wrath in the weather," he answers, and she goes on, clambering down to the path round the foot of the hill, to watch the rocks playing lacemaking with the tossing sea. Nothing happens to me when I am alone, she thinks. Miss Adams went on and on when we were reading Wordsworth, about how good for you it was, and Jenny Martin said you were only truly yourself when you were quite alone, and Miss Adams said Yes, good girl, Jenny, how true, so I ought to be really myself-est right now, at this very moment, and am

84

I? What am I? A great wave explodes in her attention, and casts a swift lace coverlet over the naked rock. I'm just not like that, that's all. I'm a mirror; I just reflect. And all sorts of things happen in a mirror when there are people moving around it, but when it's alone it's empty, glassy and still. When I'm alone I'm just a weather-watcher. Who would I be with no weather, all alone in the dark? She shudders. I just don't like being alone. I think I'll go home now, and have tea with Gran!

She turns back, and scrambles homewards over the sloping clumpy grass, till she can see the town curved round its bay, clinging to its up-and-down hillsides, stretching out towards her along what was once a sandbar, to this hill that was once really an island. She can see her grandmother's house, high on the hill overlooking; a distant four-square outline against the green-gold misty wood that caps the cliff. She settles into swift strides, and makes homewards, and so is just too late to see the *Amulet*, with Jeremy and Paul, sailing past the Island, close inshore, going to lift lobster-pots off Clodgy Point.

Looking up from hauling lobster-pots up their length of sodden rope, Paul sees the hazy shore. Above the golden sand he sees the green field of the cemetery, crowded with white headstones. There lie the ancient mariners, like a landed shoal, each with a marble marker-buoy anchored above his head. They must like to lie there, within sound of the sea, he thinks. And from out here you can see the headlands of this tall coast, stretching away east and west, shadow beyond shadow against sea and sky. And Godrevy stands out seawards, how clear and near! "Oh, couldn't we go round the lighthouse?" he says to Jeremy, though even as he says it, he struggles with the thought that he ought to wait for Madge, ought to say, keep it for another day when Madge will come too.

"Not straight from here, we can't," says Jeremy, "because of the Skerries."

"Skerries?"

"That's a rock reef. Runs west from Godrevy three mile. Look, you can see the waves on it over yonder, breaking white; and that lightbuoy marking the end of it."

But Paul can only see cormorants, floating like hooks out of the water, and then a seal, that surfaces and stares at them with huge sad mermaid eyes, then submerges in a suck of bubbles that looks like the cloudy spiral in the heart of a green glass marble.

"We'll go in with these lobsters," says Jeremy, "and then I'll take you round it." And I can find Madge on the quay, and tell her, thinks Paul, happily.

Madge walks along the quayside, round the harbour, past the custom house, and the lifeboat in its shed, and the church, and up towards the railway station. On the railway platform, suspended above the beach, people are waiting for the train. Right at the end of the platform, leaning against the notice that says *ST IVES* stands a soldier in khaki, with a girl in his arms. Her head is against his shoulder, with her bright red hair wrapped round him by the wind, and he leans his cheek down against the crown of her head, and holds her loosely, hands joined behind her back. How still they are, thinks Madge. Oh, I wonder what they feel like, standing so still! They look like a statue, or a famous painting, or a war photograph from *Picture Post*, or the last shot in a sad, sad film; yet they are only Amy, and Walt, who blushes and stammers when I speak to him, and they will be ordinary again very soon, for I hear the train puffing, coming to disturb them. She watches them stand, unmoving, while everyone else picks up cases, moves them nearer the edge of the platform, and waves, and flutters; she watches them not move till the rattling train pulls in front of them, and blocks her view.

Then she takes the short cut across the beach to reach the cliff path home. The beach is empty, except for two boys swimming, and a dog, and a man sitting alone on a bench by the changing huts. She knows both man and dog. The dog is chasing the plovers and gulls on the rocky end of the beach, barking in the distance. Ralph is sitting, head leaning back, his stick planted upright in the sand in front of him, and his hands crossed upon the handle. Very quietly Madge goes and sits down on the other end of the bench beside him. She mirrors water, rock, sand, sky, and says nothing. After a while he says,

"You are better to be with when you are happy, Madge."

"Oh!" says Madge, so startled that she jumps. "How did you know someone was here?"

"I heard you come. I felt your weight as you sat down on the bench."

"But however did you know it was me?"

"Ah. By your aura. I know it quite well by now."

"I didn't know I had one of those," says Madge. "What is it?"

"It's a sort of essence, emanating from all living things; a kind of atmosphere."

87

"You mean a *feel* about me?"

"Yes, that's it."

"And you really can feel it, and mine really truly is different from anyone elses? Oh, tell me about it! What do I feel like?"

"Aha," he says, smiling. "Why are you so pleased? Do you like having a secret essence?"

"Oh, yes, I do," says Madge, drawing her knees up to her chin, and hugging them. "I'd much rather be known by my aura than by the other way – by how I look."

"Why?" says Ralph, smiling really deeply now, turning towards her. "Aren't you pretty enough for yourself?"

"Oh, it's not that. It's just that looking is so shallow – you know, one glance, and you can tell what sort of a person *she* is; horrid! But there's Gran now – she looked so beautiful in old photographs, and now she's gone very small, and wrinkled, especially round the corners of her eyes, like gulls' footprints in the sand, but she feels just the same to be with."

"So you like your aura for its keeping qualities?"

"Yes, if it's a nice aura to begin with!"

"Rest assured that it is. It makes me feel perfectly at peace. You may safely hope for it to remain unchanged."

As the *Amulet* glides in beside the little pier by the lifeboat shed, Paul gathers her painter in one hand, and throws it upwards, unwinding in jerky flight, to one of the ageless, sunweathered, blue-clad men who linger for ever, smoking and talking on the quay, ready to catch ropes, and make a turn with them round the bollards, in return for "Good Morning" or storm-talk, or a fish or two. Paul loops his end round the post at *Amulet*'s prow, the wooden post that is scooped and grooved and sculptured with the run of the rope at a thousand landings, and, leaning back on his heels, heaves hard and slowly draws *Amulet* in towards the quay. Looking up the flight of weedy steps he sees straight overhead the tower of the church, standing so near the shore that it might almost be on the quay itself. It has four little bomb-shaped turrets, tapered top and bottom, projecting from the sides of the top of the tower; in outline against the sky it looks like a lobster claw, raised skywards.

Leaving Jeremy to unload his living lobsters, Paul scurries up the steps and looks for Madge. I must find her, he tells himself, or I shall have to ask Jeremy to go another day instead, and honestly, we've asked so often before, and he's never said yes, that I don't know how long it might be before he says yes again, so where is she, where is she now? Madge is nowhere handy, that's clear. He half-expected her to be sitting having cream tea, but she isn't, not in the nearby little shop with its cloam-oven scones, and cream-pots, and strawberry jam. Is that her, he wonders, walking along Smeaton's Quay, across the harbour? I know what! and running, groping in his pocket for sixpence, he races for the money-in-the-slot telescope perched on the harbour wall. It starts to buzz as soon as it has eaten his sixpence. He fumbles with the focus, and rakes the harbour round, searching. Oh, please, Madge, be there, he begs, for it was always Madge who wanted the lighthouse so badly, and asked to go round it, and wanted to know for certain whether it stood on one rock, as it looks from here, or two, as it looks from the beach. But though he scans all round the harbour he cannot see her. The beach – perhaps she has gone to the beach – he swings around. He can only see half the beach from here, for the nearer end is masked by houses on Pend Olva Point. There is nothing but a dog running on it – yes, there, on a bench, two people, and surely one is a girl in a white dress. He tries to make the focus change – and then, click, the sixpence runs out, and a black shutter closes across his sight. But not before he has guessed who is sitting with Madge. Oh, all *right* then! he tells himself. See if I care! and he saunters casually back to Jeremy, and says, "Ready when you are."

Looking back, as Jeremy sets a course east-north-east across the bay, Paul sees the great bulk of Rose-wall Hill, purple with dying heather, rising slowly and solemnly behind the town as they draw away seawards.

Madge watches vaguely as a boat sails out across the bay.

"I don't think what you say can be true," she says thoughtfully to Ralph.

"That your aura is a good one? Why not?"

"No, that it makes you feel perfectly at peace."

"Again, why not?"

"Well, I don't think you can feel quite like that with anyone. You're so good at knowing when people move, sensing what they're doing. And people never sit still, do they? Heads move, or maybe just eyes, but people are always looking. I should think you'd always find people restless, fidgety with seeing."

Ralph suddenly puts his hand over his eyes, as though they were capable of being seen through.

"I wonder how you know that, Madge," he says, in a quiet voice. "I wonder how you guessed that."

"I was thinking about you, then I guessed it."

"You are right. When people turn to look, it feels as though they were jiggling or tapping to some tune I cannot hear. But you are stiller than most."

"I try to be," says Madge. "I really try." But in spite of herself she looks up to see how far the boat has gone, and now she sees that it is the *Amulet*, going where no fishes are, far out, and it seems to be going towards Godrevy. They are going without me! she cries inwardly, overwhelmed with a sense of time spent, chances lost.

"We are going on Saturday," she says. "I can come and read to you twice more."

"The devil keep me from people's kindness!" says Ralph harshly. "I shall miss you."

"I haven't been kind," she says. "And there's twice more."

"You live in the present, I see."

When else is there? wonders Madge. Don't we all? In a while Ralph says, "Well, Madge, since you've brought your keen looking to haunt me, will you share it with me? Tell me what the waves look like."

"Oh, I can't," says Madge. "How can I? There aren't words for that sort of thing, not easy ones, and I'm not John Keats, or William Shakespeare."

"Try."

Madge watches first. The waves rise and run towards her in glassy straight ridges, and break, spilling froth and diamond-bright flying droplets, and spending and exhausting themselves in creamy foam; then they fall back, sleeking and glossing the yellow slope of the sand. . . . "Well," she says, "the waves

91

rise up along the edge of the sea, and run forwards, and break all frothy on the sloping sand. They make it wet and smooth."

"Thank you Madge," he says, after waiting as though she might say more.

"Oh, but I feel so bad about it!" she cries. "I feel as though I'm cheating you, selling you short. I mean, when I'm reading, you are actually getting the book; but words for waves. . . ."

"And now who's rubbing salt, Madge?" says Ralph. "I'm getting cold sitting still in the wind; I must go in. Goodbye till tomorrow, Madge. Keep your lovely aura shining bright."

And scrambling up the steep cliff path, hugging the thought of her aura, like a new toy, a new dress, a promised holiday, Madge meets Paul, running, laughing and jumping towards her from below, crying, "Madge! Madge! I've been to the lighthouse!" And a voice inside Madge that she very seldom hears, from something coiled up and hidden, deep down, wails "Too late! Too late!"

They find Gran in the kitchen, trying to cut up cheese.

"It's Amy's night out, tonight, dears. Bread and cheese for supper."

"I thought she went out the other night," said Paul. "Bread and cheese will be fine."

"Here, let me do that, Gran," says Madge, taking the knife from her, and beginning to slice the block of cheddar.

"Well, she has more nights off than Mrs Arthur used to," says Gran. "Thank you, Madge. I'm such a lot of trouble to look after nowadays, she has to work very hard. And she must see Walt, her young man, you know. He hasn't *asked* her yet, and he'll be going home to America soon."

"What's so difficult about you, Gran?" says Paul, giving her a sudden one-armed hug around the shoulders, that nearly throws her off balance.

"I'm getting old. I'm very forgetful. I forgot to ask Amy to cut up the cheese for me. I can only remember things from way back. . . ."

This is where I should ask about my father, if I were going to, thinks Madge. But whenever I ask she gets so unhappy. It must be she minds so much about "missing in the war" it has spoiled thinking about what went before. That must be it. I won't say anything. . . .

". . . there used to be much nicer cheese before the war, for instance," Gran is saying. "It wasn't always so hard. But there, there, we have to take what we can get nowadays, and be thankful."

Sitting quietly after supper, while Gran threads up a row of needles with coloured wools for her tapestry, Madge nibbles the satin-white almonds, and leaves the raisins unpartnered in the glass dish. She is curled up in the window-seat, with a great purple prospect of deepening evening and dark sea behind glass behind her. Lights shine, jewels in velvet. Two amber lights on Smeaton's Quay glow out there, one at the end, one halfway along, and the sapphire blue flare on the little quay, windows and lamp-posts between, and looking the other way the lonely golden spark of Godrevy, suspended in horizonless distance. You count to ten slowly between each flash and the next. Paul is curled in his grandfather's huge empty armchair, with his favourite book, *Clipper Ships Round the Horn*, full of finicky grey steel engravings, showing the great fine ships exactly, to the last sheet and belaying pin.

"When these ships sailed into Bristol, they must have come right past the mouth of this bay," he says.

"And perhaps a pilot went out from here to take them up-channel and home," says Madge.

"And the pilot boat would have taken unsalted meat on board, and fresh bread, and cabbages . . ."

"And brought back green-painted tins of tea, that set up the first Mr Laity in business, long ago!" They laugh.

"Find me the Home Service, for the news, dear," says Gran. But Paul finds a shipping forecast. ". . . Fastnet, Sole, Lundy, Irish Sea. Storm warning. Gale force nine. East North East. Imminent. . . ."

"That's here, isn't it?" says Paul.

"Oh dear," says Gran. "Are there any ships in the bay, Madge?"

"No, Gran."

"I really thought I saw a light when I looked up at the end of my last row."

Madge looks, but sees nothing.

"It must have been the lightbuoy on the end of the Skerries, Gran," says Paul.

"Ah well. You have sharp eyes then, for I can't spy that from here."

"Jeremy says it's a poor light, for what it warns of," says Paul, yawning, turning the knob again for the news. And by the end of the news he has fallen suddenly and deeply asleep. "How nice to be young," says Gran. "I never sleep like that nowadays. Can't seem to lie still."

Madge takes the book from Paul's slack hands, and rocks him in the chair to waken him. "Goo'-night, Gran, Madge," he mumbles, and staggers un-

94

steadily towards the stairs. "Drunk again, you pirate!" Madge calls after him.

Gran lays her work down on her knees, and looks at the fire. "I met Professor Ashton in Fore Street today," she says. "He was looking much better in himself, I thought. He says he has stopped mouldering away, and is thinking of beginning on another book."

"Good," says Madge, looking at the clippers, to hide her glowing with joy.

"But Paul – do you think he has enjoyed himself as much as usual?"

"Oh, yes, I'm sure he has."

"I just wondered what he does with himself while you're reading to Professor Ashton."

"Oh, he fishes, and swims . . . look, Gran, don't *worry* about it. The whole point about Paul is that you don't have to think about him."

"Now, whatever do you mean by that, dearie?"

"Well, some people – my friend Jenny at school, for instance – if you just happen to want to do something different one lunch-hour, or if you just happen not to have gone and found them at break for a day or two, or you didn't keep a peppermint humbug for them, suddenly they're less friends than they were; you have to keep looking after your friendship with them. But Paul's more like a brother – I mean like I imagine a brother would have been if only I had had one – he's just there, and he doesn't go away whatever you do. I mean, we just don't have to keep together all the time to be in with each other."

"Oh, I see," says Gran, taking up her needlework again. "As long as you're sure, dearie."

"Oh, listen to the wind getting up," says Madge. "There really is a storm coming. How quickly the weather changes here! I sometimes think I'd better wait till Paul's old enough, and marry him."

"Oh?" says Gran, looking up at Madge, really startled.

"Well, because I know where I am with him. Anyone else would need so much – what's that that houses need done to them? – you know, so much maintenance work."

"Go along with you!" says Gran, crossly. "Stuff and nonsense! Time for bed, dearie."

Madge goes to bed quicker than to sleep. A wind is buffeting the house, roaring. Through her shut windows it pokes cold fingers, and billows the curtains. Madge remembers, words and tune together, the morning assembly hymn: *Virgin most Pure, Star of the Sea, Pray for the Mariner, Pray for Me. . . .* Oh, do that will you, if you're really there? she says. For truly, there is wrath in the weather now. Even from her room, looking into the trees, surely she can hear the sea! How it roars! Slipping from her bed, lifting the curtain aside to look out, she sees the branches of the great chestnut tree flailing and tossing like willow. Is it waves I hear, or only the agony of the leaves? she wonders. Oh, I'm glad to be indoors! Up beyond Tregenna Hill lightning shows, as though the dark wall of the sky had quaked, and cracked for a moment, and shown the fire beyond. Snuggling back into her warm bed she murmurs, *Blow wind, and crack your cheeks!* I'm safe, I'm warm. . . .

Not the wind, but silence wakes her. Rising she opens the curtains upon a sky windswept and rain-washed, pale, fresh with the first new light. The ground below the tree is covered with newly-fallen copper and gold. Surely I am awake before Paul *this* time! she thinks, and pulling on her blue dressing-gown she goes barefoot up the stairs to see.

He is there, a hump in the blanket and a tuft of fair hair on the pillow, unstirring. She sits on the other bed to wait for him. Out of his high window she looks at the sea, dark, rolling smoothly and washed with shifting pools of silver reflected from the pale sky. But she is very soon cold, sitting in her thin nightdress under her worn dressing-gown. She begins to shiver, as though all that cold brightness outside had chilled her. Turning back the quilt on the spare bed, she slips into it, and pulls the covers round her chin, and watches for Paul to wake. And sleep creeps up on her again.

Opening her eyes suddenly, she looks into Paul's. "You're here," he says, propping himself up on one arm, looking and smiling. For a moment she has forgotten that it isn't last year, and she doesn't wake every morning under the whitewashed eaves with him. Then, "I woke up before you, for once, and came for you," she says, proudly.

"Coming out?" says Paul, getting up, throwing off his pyjama jacket.

"I'll get some clothes," she says, going.

They have to throw back the bolts on the door, and unlock the chain, having beaten Amy downstairs this one morning. The garden is cool and dewy, and chills their sandalled feet. "The wind will have brought down some conkers now, Paul, surely," says Madge, and off they run to the grove to look. In a thick crunchy carpet of leaves lie hundreds of the green spiky globes. They try to prise them open, with blunt fingers. Treading on them gently squeezes open the reluctant shells, but the conkers inside are not ready yet; they have creamy patches, like those glossy brown and white cows. It takes Paul a little while to find one that is brown all over, dark and polished, and finely-veined with lines of deeper brown, like contours on a map. He pockets it.

"Shall we go to the beach?" asks Madge. This morning air is cool like water, she thinks, nearly but not quite shivering. Walking is like swimming now, with an is-it-too-cold-or-isn't-it, well-when-you've-been-in-a-few-moments-it's-nice sort of pleasant chill all over me.

They let themselves out through the gate in the garden wall, onto the zig-zag path. At the second turn it branches, going one way to the wide sands of the public beach, and the other to their own small cove with its little shelf of sand. They stop to pick watery blackberries from the crowded brambles along the path. Looking back at the big beach, and the town, Madge sees the seaward side of Smeaton's Quay, with the waves breaking on it and bursts of foam climbing up it. In a great sweeping half-circle the waves are rolling onto the beach and harbour, as though the sea remembered the storm, even if the morning weather had forgotten. She notices that there is a lot of driftwood on the beach. Then they turn to go down to their own beach, and seeing the crag of Godrevy standing out deep and clear against the more shadowy headlands beyond, Madge says, "Paul, what was the lighthouse like?"

"Great," says Paul.

"Oh, *tell* me!" she says, "please."

"It isn't round," he says, "though it looks it from here. When you get there it has eight sides. It looks very solid, sort of standing eight-square. And there are two rocks. You can see right through the cleft, with the water boiling between them. And there's a garden on the lighthouse rock."

"A garden?" says Madge, astonished.

"Yes. There's a wall thrown round it, like a loop of rope on the steep slope east of the lighthouse, and inside it is a garden."

"What kind of a garden?" says Madge entranced. She tries to imagine it. "Oh, it must be beautiful!"

"Well, with flowers and things," says Paul. "What else would there be? And then round the other side there's a little quay, and a breeches-buoy, and a scatter of rocks."

"But the garden . . ." Madge begins, her inward eye flowering like the rock with the thought of it, but then she realises it is no good asking Paul. He can't tell me what *I* would have felt to see it. . . . I would only get words for waves . . . and she runs after him down the path.

"Oh, look!" says Madge. "The sea has made a cliff of sand." The storm has bulldozed the beach, and raised a precipice knee-high all along it. They run; the edge of the sand steep crumbles and collapses under their feet.

"Hey, look at the boat, Madge," says Paul as they come up to it. It lies now tilting steeply, for the storm waves have lifted it out of the sand. From the twists in the chain, and the distance it has moved they can see it has been rolled over and over, emptied of sand, freed from the wet weight and gritty clasp of it. Had the high tide washed only a foot or so further the boat would have smashed on the rocks, being wave-handled like that. Instead, it perches on the shore at a rakish angle, with the smug look of a survivor. "Great!" says Paul. "It's free!" He grips the stern and heaves, and the boat slides a little on the firm wet sand. "We can paint it all over now," he says. "We'd never have dug it right out ourselves." But Madge isn't looking or listening. She is staring at the far end of the beach, under the lee of the point, for beside the cliff of sand there, something is washed up, lying.

"Oh, what's that?" she murmurs.

"It's a drowned man," says Paul.

"Oh, it can't be!" Madge says. "He's resting, that's all. He's swum so far he's resting, isn't he?"

"Come on," says Paul.

"No, I don't think. . . ."

"We have to go and see," he says, starting.

I'm afraid to see someone dead, thinks Madge. What will it be like? She reaches for Paul's hand at the same moment as he reaches for hers. But when they come up to the man she is not frightened. He is as empty and silent as a shell. The sand has washed into the creases in his clothes, and into his hair. His arms are thrown up beside his head, as though the beach were his pillow. He has lost one shoe. His eyes shine with emptiness, like those of a fish. They are open and blind. And remembering when the fish seem to be dead they suddenly flap and thump, Madge shudders and whimpers, and clings to Paul, hiding her face in his shirt.

"Oh, let go, Madge, do!" says Paul, "Look, there's the lifeboat, and we ought to wave to it."

The lifeboat is chugging past the beach, near inshore, with everyone aboard her scanning the line of the coast. Taking off his shirt, and instantly goosey in the sharp morning air, Paul shouts and waves it like a flag. Madge shouts too. "Here he is!" Paul cries, "Here!" and the boat turns, and noses towards them, and comes aground with a crunch, and the lifeboat men jump out. One of them is Jeremy, Madge sees, half-hidden by the brim of his sou'-wester, and wearing thigh-boots that make him walk with a roll. They are all just the fishermen, dressed for storms. They stand round the body.

"He's a goner, then," says the captain. "Anyone know him, just for the book?"

"I do," says the man from behind the counter in the fishermen's Co-operative. "'E's that Frenchy, come back for his paint."

"That makes the eight of them, then, all found," says the captain. "Let's have him, boys, and then we can go in for a bite of breakfast." Four of them lean down, and pick up the dead man, head and foot. "You know what 'is name was, Tom?" says the captain as they heave the man's floppy weight over the gunwale of the lifeboat.

"No. It were gobbledygook to me, that's for sure. But it'll be in my order book, like as not."

"After breakfast then, you'll look it out for me," says the captain. "And you, young feller, you did well to wave us in. We couldn't see him from out there, with the waves breaking between. You saved us hours of beating to and fro."

He puts a hand on the boat, but Jeremy says, "Hold it. They're troubled maybe. They're only childer."

The captain comes over to Paul and Madge, and says, "Now don't you be fretted by seeing of him. He were a trawlerman, and for the most part fisher-folk don't ever learn to swim, that the drowning if

101

it come may be quick and easy. Nothing terrible to it."

"But what happened?" asks Paul.

"They wouldn't come in to shelter last night," says the captain. "They dragged anchor, and went onto the point yonder. Ship broke up at once. We got most of them out of the water alive, which is more than they deserve, but then we were all ready to come out for them when we saw they were meaning to ride the storm out in the bay. Now you make off home, the pair of you, and get a bite to eat to cheer you; the lass looks in need of it, and so am I."

And Madge does look awfully cheesy, thinks Paul, taking her hand and leading her away. They hear the engine of the lifeboat start again, but they do not look back. A man is dead, thinks Madge. Dead. And we have *seen* it. No wonder I feel cold. But I couldn't eat, I really couldn't.

"I'm jolly hungry," says Paul. "Aren't you?"

"No," says Madge. "I feel funny inside, like sea-sick."

"A bite to cheer you, the captain said," says Paul. "Give it a try."

And the awful thing is, thinks Madge, a little later, licking the butter from hot toast off her fingers, and listening to Paul telling Gran all about it, and to Gran saying, "Dear, oh dear," that it *has* cheered me. There must be something wrong with me. I must really be vulgar and shallow like Jenny Martin said I was.

"I think I'll go and get the paint now," says Paul, getting up.

"But there wasn't any the right—" Madge begins.

102

"There was lots saved for the Frenchman, and he won't want it now," says Paul. "See you later."

"How dreadful for you," says Ralph. "It must have blighted your morning. And a sunny one too. It seems this summer will never end."

"Oh, but the weather has gone different. There is a haze in the air, and the leaves are all golden on the trees now. What shall I read today?"

"It's an Alice day, today. Do you remember, we had left her in the shady wood, where things had no names?"

"Oh, yes," says Madge, opening the book at her mark, and reading on. *Just then a Fawn came wandering by; it looked at Alice with its gentle large eyes, but didn't seem at all frightened. "Here then! Here then!" Alice said, as she held out her hand and tried to stroke it; but it only started back a little, and then stood looking at her again.*

"What do you call yourself?" the Fawn said at last. Such a soft sweet voice it had!

"I wish I knew!" thought poor Alice. She answered rather sadly, "Nothing, just now."

"Think again," it said: "that won't do."

Alice thought, but nothing came of it. "Please would you tell me what you *call yourself?" she said timidly. "I think that might help a little."*

"I'll tell you, if you come a little further on," the Fawn said. "I can't remember HERE."

So they walked on together through the wood,

Alice with her arms clasped lovingly round the soft
neck of the Fawn, till they came out into another
open field, and here the Fawn gave a sudden bound
into the air, and shook itself free from Alice's arm.
"I'm a Fawn!" it cried out in a voice of delight.
"And dear me! you're a human child!" A sudden look
of alarm came into its beautiful brown eyes, and in
another moment it had darted away at full speed....

From where she is sitting, Madge can see Paul, on
the beach, below her, naked to the waist, bending
over the boat, with a brush loaded blue-green; she
can see the tiny splash of colour on the brush; she
can see the spreading brilliance on the old worn
sides of the boat. I am happy, she thinks. I am here,
with Ralph. My voice solaces him. But I, I can see
Paul, and blue-green, and sea, and the lighthouse,
far away.

"Madge," says Ralph, in the pause her dreaming
has made, in the book, "you have been reading to
me all this time, and I don't know what you look
like. I should like to know, before you go away
tomorrow. Will you let me?"

"How could you know that?" says Madge, surprised. "Will I let you what?"

"Let me touch you."

"Yes," she says, putting down the book, and going
towards him. She is not quite sure what he wants.
Reaching out in front of him, he gropes for her.
Then, finding her hands, he pulls her down towards
him, till she kneels on the grass in front of his chair,
between his knees. He tilts her chin, upturning her
face towards him, and covers her over with both his
hands outspread. His fingertips press gently on her
temples, run along the line of her eyebrows, across
the lids of her eyes, weighing them down, and

lingering at the outer corners. His cobweb touch weaves over her, finding the shape of her cheekbone, and the turn of her jawbone, tracing down to her chin, running to and fro across her lips, and then he seems to have done, and holds her still, hands cupped round her chin.

"Well?" she says, starting to laugh with a smile, and at once his fingers catch the lips and swelling cheek muscles of her smile and hold it frozen, dying away under his hands.

"You are younger than I supposed," he says, a little sadly. "Far younger."

"I feel quite grown-up to me," she says. He lets his hands fall, to her shoulders, and then to his knees. He has done with her. But carried away by the abandoned and generous feeling that lending him her face has aroused in her, Madge puts her arms round his neck, and kisses him swiftly as she rises and moves away.

"Madge. Dear girl," he says, half-deploring, half-amused. "Back to work. I want more of the horrible book now," and Madge pulls a face at the front cover of *Seven Types of Ambiguity* and reads on steadily, raising her eyes at the end of each paragraph to watch the spread of colour over the boat, down below, beyond the gulls' cries, and the blackberry tangles on the cliff. The book drones on and on.

Coming home towards lunch, through the trees ablaze with fiery gold, rustling her feet through the leaf-fall, Madge thinks One More Day. Only one more day, and the thought of it hits her, the moment has come, which always comes at Goldengrove, when you must remember that you are only here on holiday, briefly, by permission. The going-home journey lurches into Madge's mind: the train chuffing round under the cliff, under the trees she walks through now, along the rocky coast. The sea-shallows, all green, and blotched with purple where the rocks run under water, and Godrevy, queen of the distance, still in view, and then another long golden beach with surf breaking, breaking white, and then, beyond a second headland, the great expanse of Porthkidney sands, wide and pale, with great lines of long surf rolling onto it. And then the train turns inland under Lelant church on the height, and there is a marshy estuary, and mud, and derelict buildings, and the landscape all chewed and uglified with the overgrown heaps from the tin mining. But beyond St Erth, looking back full of regret and feeling the uprooting in your heart, you catch just for one moment, one glimpse, through the gap where the river goes out to sea, far off, the shape of the town, and the colour of it, and then it has gone. And worse than ever this time, because of what will he do without me? thinks Madge. He will walk round in his dark, and do without voices, and do without books, and never be able to work or think again. And for the first time in her life, she thinks all for herself, and unprompted by anyone, how cruel life is. Poor Ralph; even Mr Rochester got his sight back when he had someone to love and look after him properly, and Ralph has no one. Swimming in sadness, she goes in to her lunch.

Across her plate is a letter from home, addressed in her mother's carefully elaborate hand. All through lunch the letter lurks by her side-plate, lying in wait for her afternoon.

"Don't come yet, Madge," says Paul, bolting his

rice-pudding, with a streak of paint on his cheek, and lots under his fingernails. "Give me an hour, and then come and see it as a surprise."

So Madge takes her letter and goes off walking to read it. Something warns her to take it somewhere special, as though to disinfect it, to overpower it with the feel of some good place. So she goes along the cliff path to the Huer's house, where she hasn't been yet this year. It is a little white-washed shelter, high among the trees on the cliff face, overlooking the bay. And here, long ago, the Huer sat, ready to make a hue-and-cry after pilchards, when he saw them in the bay. He made tick-tack signals with green branches in his hands, and the fishermen ran to their black-tarred boats, that were drawn up at the back of all the beaches, and rowed away after the millions of silver fishes.

"But they don't come no more," Jeremy said, "no man knows whyfore." And, "Jeremy, *how* can a man on the cliff see pilchards?" Paul asked, last year, or the year before. "Do they swim near the top?"

"They make an oily mark," said Jeremy. "See this water here, wind-rough? Well, the pilchards are swimming eight, maybe ten feet down, in their 'undreds and thousands, and the pull of them makes the water sudden smooth."

Madge sits down on the Huer's bench, and looks for oily marks for a long time before she opens her letter.

Dear Madge, it goes,

Your Grandmother has telephoned me in some distress and told me that she thinks you must now be told the whole truth about your father. I had hoped to keep it from you a little while yet, but it seems that something you have been saying to her about Paul has made your Grandmother believe that it is urgent. I have always told you that your father was missing in the war, and so he was in a way. He is missing as far as you or I are concerned because during the war he decided he could not stay with me any longer, but that he wanted to marry someone else. Please believe me that although he thought this was my fault, I did not, and we are not the first or only people to find ourselves in this sort of mess. Usually when such a thing happens the children of the marriage stay with their mother, but your father absolutely would not agree to part with his son, even though Paul was little more than a baby at the time. He felt very strongly that he wanted to bring up his son himself, and he made me believe that if I opposed him in this he would ask the court to let him take you too, and that they might agree. Of course, he had a home to offer, and a new mother waiting in the wings, and I had nothing. Because I was afraid of losing both of you, I let him take Paul without a fight. The two of us agreed not to subject ourselves to more pain and upset by allowing visits to either child. Especially once you had a loving step-father I thought it would upset you less not to know anything about it. So you see, Madge dear, it is natural for you to love Paul, indeed it is your duty, for he is your brother. But he can never be anything else to you. I hope, as I have always hoped for him, that he is well and happy, and that you are both enjoying your stay with your Grandmother. We will meet the 3.30 into Paddington on Saturday.

Your loving Mother

Looking up, Madge sees the bay, briefly, wind-streaked rough and smooth, as though the shoals had come back, and she was the first to see them. A little knot of pain and anger lies within her like a stone. Then suddenly tears spout from her eyes, floods of them, and everything goes blurry. "Oh damn!" she says, rubbing them fiercely away. "Why do I always do that!" and why, she thinks, couldn't Mummy leave me alone, at least while I'm here? Lying to me like that, lying to me night and day, for years and years, without so much as a flicker in her china-blue eyes, and then suddenly not being able to wait, blurting out suddenly like milk spilling, and hiding behind Gran and hiding behind writing letters! It isn't till the day after tomorrow I go home, and she has stolen my day here away from me, and I hate her! But no raging against her mother can stop the thought *He wanted Paul, and he didn't want me.*

"Well, I won't care," she tells herself defiantly. "Other people do want me." She gets up, and goes back towards Goldengrove, leaving the letter to blow away, and catch on a thorn, and wave there like a flag.

Gran is sitting on the terrace, dozing, under her rug, and she has forgotten to drink her cup of tea. The lemon slice floats around in it, going brown unregarded.

"Hullo, dearie," she says, waking up when Madge sits down at her feet.

"Oh, Gran, I don't want to go home," says Madge. "Couldn't I stay here?"

"You're not going yet, child," says Gran. "There's tomorrow. Still tomorrow."

"Oh, but tomorrow's not enough, Gran. I'm not just saying it; I'm asking with all my heart. Please, Gran, I really need to stay."

"There, there, dearie. There's no use fretting at
what must be. You can come back next year, as
usual." And, how violent people are, before they're
old, she thinks to herself. That sly, selfish woman has
managed to tell her at last, then, and the letter has
upset the child. . . . Well, what could be expected,
after all, what did they imagine would come of it?
Perhaps I should not have said anything . . . not
meddled with it at all . . . but it had to come sooner
or later, had to come out, sooner or later had to be
told . . . there is no escape from the truth. And now
she troubles me with all this not wanting to go. . . .
I daresay things aren't what they ought to be at
home, for her. I never approved of all that; I think I
remember I never liked her mother at all much. But
how the child takes on! "Try not to take life so hard,
dearie," she says to Madge. "You must take things
as they come."

And lose them as they go, I suppose, thinks Madge
bitterly. And she wanders away under the tall trees,
where the strawberries have been, and where now
there is a russet carpet to kick through, and a view
through the thinning mosaic curtains of shades of
gold, to blue beyond, to sea and sky. At the end of
the little wood where the land plunges downwards,
and she can look through the last trees out to sea,
Madge sits.

Well, who does want me? she thinks. They want
me, in a distant way at school, where the teachers
like me, and like the things I say, and Jenny Martin
does too, most of the time. But not really at home
any more. I feel as if I were always trying to squeeze
into a place too small for me; I feel that all the time
at home. I am always a burden to them, especially to
him. I cannot do anything they find pleasant and

110

useful. Only one person has ever found me useful, is that why I love him so? What I really want is to stay with him. I could keep his house orderly, and take him for walks, and talk to him, and read, and write down his books for him. How happy he would be! I would need nothing else. Shutting her eyes she sees the dedication page of his great book: *To Margaret, without whose unfailing help this book could never have been written.* Grander still, she dreams, a book of his famous letters, his famous words, edited by herself, with a brief biographical note, written by herself. And she can't avoid thinking how much easier that would be than passing her own exams, and doing something of her own. And, she thinks, I could look at the sea every day. And it can't be quite time to go and look at Paul's boat yet; I'll go and ask Ralph about it now.

The roses round his cottage door are ragged; a wind-scatter of leaves litters the lawn. She walks through the unlatched door, and finds him sitting alone by the window, fingering his book in braille.

"Hullo?" he says, surprised.

"I've come to tell you that I'm not going home, Ralph," she says. "So I shall be able to read to you more than once more, after all. I shall read to you every day."

"What's happened?" he asks. "Are you staying on with your grandmother?"

"No," says Madge. "I can't make Gran see that I have to stay. So if I'm not going away, I will have to stay here, with you."

"And I'll wrap you in a blanket at night, and put you in the attic room, and you will come creeping down, I suppose, and read to me when no one's about," he says, smiling gently. "What a splendid

111

idea, Madge. What a shame we can't really."

"But I mean it, Ralph! Why can't we really?"

"Oh, you know we can't, dear girl. You can't be serious."

"But I am, I am. How will you manage without me? What will you do? I can't bear to think of you, alone in silence and dark, so I think I had better not leave you."

"Oh my God," he says flatly. Then after a pause, "I shall manage, Madge, as I managed before you came. I shall pay someone to read to me."

"How horrible!" cries Madge. "You know that wouldn't be the same! Why shouldn't I stay with you?"

"What would people think? What would they say?"

"You sound like my mother! I can't believe you give a damn about that. I don't."

"Well then, in the second place," he says, speaking quietly, in a grey kind of voice, "because you wouldn't really stay. You'd quickly get tired of it, and go. Why should I expose myself to that?"

"If you let me stay, I will stay," says Madge simply. "I will stay for ever."

"Madge, do you remember reading Milton to me? Milton went blind. He had daughters, and they had to read his books for him, day after day. And they hated him for it. It is a well-known thing that they hated him for it."

"I couldn't hate you," Madge declares, unshakeably. "Not if there were twenty horrible books to be got through every week."

"Who in hell do you think you are!" he cries, jumping up, and beginning to pace the room. He stumbles on a table, and then, groping, goes and leans against the window as though he were looking out. "Listen, Madge. I had a wife once. She was a good and generous person. When I went blind she left me. If she couldn't stand it, what makes you think you could? I know she wouldn't have gone if she could have helped it . . . it must be unendurable . . . I often wonder how much of what I am is blindness, and how much is me. . . . And you would lighten my darkness, would you? Just some sweet shallow child could walk in here, and do what she could not do? Do you think I could believe that?"

"I would love you," says Madge miserably, uncomprehending. "I would read to you. I would tell you what the weather looks like every day. Wouldn't that help?"

"Oh my God," he says again, clenching his fists. "Life is very hard on me. I am so lonely. And I allow myself a little pleasure, just a little pleasure in a few hours of human company, and now look what happens! Listen, Madge, you have misread me. You have been very kind, though God knows, I warned you against it. And I have liked having you here, but there was nothing personal in it. Not *you*, you understand, but just your eyes and voice. I am sorry about this, but learn from it not to be so trusting, and some day you may even look back and thank me for it. You see, Madge, nobody can be trusted. People only love, or sacrifice themselves, to serve some need of their own. When my wife left me I came to see that it is wrong to expect anything from anybody. The best of us cannot be trusted with another's happiness."

Madge hears him out and says nothing. She stares at his hollow face, with emptiness where eyes should be, and pain-lines at the corners of mouth and eyes.

113

"Madge, dear," he says after a while, "you are wrong to trust me. I am not going to trust you."

"Oh, Ralph," she says dismayed. "Something much worse than going blind has happened to you!"

"What could be worse?" he says, morosely.

"Something worse *has*! You are all full of locked doors marked *No Kindness* and *Reading Voices Only* and not letting people help, not believing they will!"

"Madge, some wounds cannot be healed, some things are beyond helping, and cannot be put right. That's just how it is."

"So even if I loved you, that wouldn't help?"

"I have liked your company, Madge. You have a lovely voice. But even if you loved me, I wouldn't trust you, or wish to rely on you."

"That's it – that's what's worse – feeling like that is worse than darkness!"

"Oh that, Madge," he says, shrugging his shoulders. "That happens to everyone. That's called growing up."

"It won't happen to me," says Madge.

It won't happen to me, she weeps, going back through the trees towards the house. She throws herself down, and lies in the leaves weeping, till she feels sick, and dizzy with the force of her sobs. Then she remembers that she was supposed to be going to meet Paul on the beach, and she gets up, and staggers towards the cliff path. Coming this way to the gate, through the thickest part of the wood where

114

rhododendron and escallonia grow rampant under the high branches and bamboo plants make little clumps of jungle, she passes the wooden hut where the boat is laid up in winter, and, with the instinct of a sick animal going to ground, she opens the door, and goes in, to cry in it. In the dry dusty gloom, however, her tears dry up, and she sits, staring aimlessly, sore-eyed. And, a broken heart really does *hurt*! she thinks, astonished, for really I am in pain, in bodily pain under my breastbone, and I always thought it was only a figure of speech. And it's a dreadful oppressive sort of pain, much worse than toothache, because where is the medicine for it, and how could it be healed? It is like that awful lurching sickness that comes when you realise you are actually hurt badly; like the moment you find that your leg is not sprained but broken, or see that the cut is deep and will need stitches. Not me, but Paul. Not me, but my lovely voice.

Vaguely her idle eyes notice that she is staring at something like a huge umbrella – a pole with cloth rolled round two-thirds of its length. She doesn't know what it is. She doesn't care what anything is. But at last she puts out a hand, and pulls at it. A triangle of faded brown-red cloth starts to unwind from the pole. It is the mast and sail from the little boat. Funny, she thinks, I didn't know it had a sail, and yet I do know, exactly. She tries to lift it, expecting it to be very heavy, but it isn't much heavier than an oar, and she drags it easily enough away from its cobwebby corner, and over towards the light. It takes several tries to pick it up ready to carry, for the way to do it is to get it onto her shoulder, nicely balanced, and it is thicker and heavier at the bottom end, so most of the length has to be in front of her, with her hand on it steadying it. It won't happen to me, Madge tells herself, starting carefully down the cliff path with her burden.

Paul has long since gone home, given her up. A pale afternoon silvers the silken sea. A quiet tide tosses and whispers on the sand. Smooth gentle waves roll in a great curve onto the beaches, like liquid emerald flowing, like liquid sapphire. Madge puts down the mast beside the boat and rests from carrying it. The ache that isn't after all a figure of speech is still with her. In a while she gets up, and tries to fit the mast into the boat. You have to slide it into the socket with the mast held at a slant that exactly matches the tilt of the boat, and it takes her several tries. When it is in she sees a little peg dangling, fixed to the foot of the mast on a frayed loop of rope, and she sees it is meant to go through both socket and mast, for a hole is drilled for it. She turns the mast in the socket till the peg will go through. Then she walks round and round the boat, with the sheet in her hand, unwinding the sail. Then she pushes and heaves the boat to move it down to the water. Paul's blue-green tacky paint comes off on her hands. But although it seems, since the storm freed it, to be riding high and easy on the slope of the sand, the boat is hard to move. Madge has to squat down with her back to the stern, and lean her full weight on it, pushing with her feet, before it shifts. But once it has started to move she can keep it moving, leaning her shoulder against it, down to the water's edge. And there the waves lift it, and the tilt suddenly straightens, and the mast swings upright, with the sail flapping on it. Giving one more thrust to the stern Madge wades after it, up to her waist in the cool water, and clambers over the side. She catches the sheet at the corner of the sail, and sits holding it, and the sail billows and pulls, and the boat moves out quite quickly on the calm water. A sudden joy sweeps away the pain that has oppressed her. I am going back, thinks Madge. I will go to Godrevy, I will see the garden on the rock, and the great light shining out. . . .

She shivers in her wet clothes, in the cold open air. A light gust of sea-breeze tugs the sail, and it tears into ribbons, the rotten fabric splitting without a sound. The rags of sail flutter and pull, and the boat moves more slowly now, feeling heavy and sluggish in the water. And it's more than wet socks and sandals Madge suddenly feels round her ankles; the boat is half full of the sea. Suddenly panic-struck, looking round at the dark shore far behind her, Madge leans abruptly forwards, to reach the empty paint tin, and bail with it, and feels her weight take her feet right through the sodden rotten wood of the bottom of the boat. It won't, she tells herself, sinking. It won't happen. . . .

"I suppose she's still waiting for me on the beach," says Paul, when Madge isn't there for tea. "I'll go and look for her."

He sees first that the boat has gone, and then he sees Madge, lying huddled and wet on the shining sand, where the Frenchman lay that morning. He walks steadily and slowly towards her, and looks down at her pallid face, pillowed on the beach, and her sand-laden, seaweed hair. Her left arm lies along her body, with paint on the upturned palm, all that is left to show for the boat. "Bloody girls!" says Paul. *Bloody girls!* I spend hours and hours on that boat, nearly all my time here, and she hardly helped at all, and it was lovely, the best thing to play in I have ever had, and all she can think to do with it is *this*! "Get up, Madge!" he says savagely, nudging her with his foot. "Oh please, do get up!" Madge opens her eyes, and with a slight convulsion vomits sea-water. She groans, and sits up, and vomits again.

"What the hell did you do that for?" says Paul, staring at her coldly.

"I wanted to drown, I think," says Madge, emptying water out of her shoe. "Or – I remember now – I wanted to sail to Godrevy."

"Sail?" says Paul, "You found a sail for her? Well if that's the mast, sticking just out of the water out there, you didn't go nearly far out enough. That water's too shallow to drown in, especially since you can swim perfectly well, Madge, you know you can. Get up and come home; you look cold."

"Don't be angry, Paul. Paul, I'm sorry about the boat."

"I am angry," he says. "I can't not be it. And it's not the boat it's about, it's you."

Half-way up the cliff path he says, "Here, Madge, put my sweater on." She is shivering, and seems hardly able to walk. He pulls one of her arms across his shoulders, winds his free arm round her waist, and brings her on. Her trembling shakes him. Why this? Why this? he thinks. Oh, Madge, you should have stayed and played with me. I love you better than anyone.

Then he has pulled her through the door, and

118

she stands leaning on him, dripping water on the tiled hall floor, and he calls loudly for Gran and Amy.

"It was an accident," he tells them later, when Madge is safely in bed. "The bottom of the boat was rotten. I knew that. But she went down when I wasn't there, and tried to sail it . . . it was an accident."

"Everything in life is that," says Gran. And I remember the last time that boat was used, she thinks, when Madge's father took her, and she was a very small child then, and sailed all the way to . . .

"She *said* she was going to Godrevy," Paul chimed in, "though she knows you forbade us to launch the boat."

"To Godrevy," says Gran, in an exasperated voice. "Oh, Paul, she needs her father. She needs your father. Say what they like, they were needed where they were."

"So she *is* my sister," says Paul. "I always thought so. But we're not supposed to know about it, are we?"

Gran shakes her head. She is rocking fiercely in her old chair to comfort herself. "Storms, storms," she says, "they touch me no longer. I am home and dry. But my heart bleeds for those who are out in them still!"

"The wind has dropped now, Gran, and the night is calm," says Paul. "Never fear, Gran."

"I have no fear for you, Paul dear," she says. "None for you."

All ready to go, Paul stands beside his bulging holdall in the hall, and restively lets Amy brush his fair, sunbleached head. Mr Arthur stands waiting with the car outside the door.

"Goodbye, dearie, come again soon," says Gran, kissing him. "Don't worry. It's only a chill, and she'll be over it in no time."

"Wish I had caught one too!" he said, smiling ruefully. "'Bye, Gran."

Going slowly – she always goes slowly nowadays – upstairs to her room, Gran watches. She can see below her, beside the beach, the little railway lines running along to the station. As she watches, Paul comes onto the platform, waves, and climbs into the train. It gathers breath, and chuffs along, sending smoke balls up over the garden, as it goes. Gran goes along then to the spare room, where Madge lies in bed, weeping. "What's the matter?" Gran asks, sitting in the chair beside the bed.

"All the golden leaves are blowing down," says Madge, looking at the branches outside the window.

"They are lovely while they last," says Gran, "aren't they?"

In a little while the doctor comes. He arrives looking cheerful, saying, "Well, well, you've grown a good deal since the year you had measles here, and even more since mumps!" But he soon looks grave. "There's a feverish chill, and a rheum in the lungs," he tells Gran, "as you usually find with people who've been in the water. There's also the shock to her system – nervous shock, you know. And the fever may get worse before it's better. We must watch her carefully and keep her quiet."

"Shall I send for her mother?" Gran asks, in

Madge's hearing, on the landing, beyond the door ajar.

"Well now," says the doctor carefully, "above all she needs peace; no excitements, no upsets. You must judge for yourself."

When the fever gets worse Madge's mother does come, briefly, down on the overnight sleeper to Penzance, and back on the afternoon train, and Madge tossing and talking to herself hardly remembers at all; only when she wakes up suddenly cool and peaceful, and feeling very weak, there are flowers and grapes in the room, and a huge box of chocolates, though they turn out to be all plain chocolate, and Madge likes only milk ones. Pity Paul's not here, she thinks, and gives them to Amy.

The evenings draw in. Amy lights fires behind the mica windows of the stove in the bedroom. The harbour lights, the squat one halfway along Smeaton's Quay, and the tall one at the end of it, and the brilliant blue flare on the end of the little pier, all light up earlier and earlier each day. And like a low-hovering golden star, Godrevy answers them. The weather is soft; watery, washed with pale colours. Every few days the doctor comes with his gold watch chain looped across in front of him, and sees Madge, and takes her pulse, and at last lets her get out of bed, though not into the open air.

Down in the warm kitchen Amy sits with Walt, wearing her diamond engagement ring, looking at America on a map. "You should have heard her when she was feverish," she tells him, "talking to herself, rambling on about the lumber room, and shut doors, and reading to that Professor. I don't know what hasn't been going on there. Educated, posh people that ought to know better so stupid and cruel you'd not believe it."

Day follows day. Madge looks out of windows, and reads. Her teachers send her bundles of books from the school library, and brisk sympathetic letters. She seems very limp and uninterested. She looks pale. The doctor tells Gran that depression following a shock to the system is common and never permanent; Gran frets at Madge's small appetite, at her pale cheeks, and gets Jeremy to send mackerel for breakfast. The year drifts into winter. An icy pallor hangs in bleached distances over the sea. Nothing happens. Madge gazes out of windows.

Then at last something happens. Paul comes. He rings on the door a little after the three o'clock train has puffed in, and comes in, still unwinding his scarf, to say, "Hullo, Madge! I came to see you."

Madge seems not to have enough energy to be surprised, but she is pleased. The first smile, the first real smile Gran has seen in a long while, spreads over her face.

"Hullo, Paul," she says. He has come straight from school, and looks oddly adult and smart in his school shirt and tie. "Gran says you're allowed to go out today, if you want to," he says. "Will you come to the beach with me, Madge?"

"Oh, yes!" she says, jumping up, and clearly they have it all planned, for here is Amy, smiling, coming with her coat held out for her, and Gran with her scarf and gloves. So the two of them go down through the rose garden, where a few frozen roses, unopened, forlornly survive, and out of the back gate, brushing past the hedge of escallonia that even in this chill moist weather gives a trace of its hot spicy summer smell. Down through the tangle of brambles beside the path, hand in hand, to the lonely sands, with their scatter of weed and shell, and a winter glaze on the water, and a winter harshness in the voice of the waves. Once there Paul runs and shouts, and finds a stone to throw into the sea, and Madge smiling, hands in pockets, walks after him.

He looks round at her, and sees overhead the cottage on the cliff. "Has that Professor guy been to see you?" he asks.

"Once or twice. A bit embarrassing really. He's gone back to London now."

"Does he write?"

"No, he just sent me a book with this in," and she brings from her pocket a crumpled printed slip of paper, decorated with printer's flowers, and bearing the words *With the Author's compliments.*

"Ugh!" says Paul, "I always did think he was a creep!"

"Yes, didn't you!" she says, smiling again, wanly.

"Did they tell you," he asks, looking at his feet, and kicking the sand, "that I'm really your brother?"

"Yes."

"I think I always knew, really, but you didn't seem to. Are you glad, Madge?"

"It's too late, Paul," she says, gazing out to sea. "It was cruel of them not to tell us all that long time when I really needed you, when I wanted a brother so badly . . . but now it's too late. It just made me feel as if I had lost you, too."

"Oh, come off it, Madge," he protests. "It got me here, for a start. I said, 'If she's my sister I'm seeing her whenever I like, and starting now, I'm going to

123

go down and see her, because she's ill.' And they just looked helplessly at each other, and said yes. So here I am."

"I'm glad you're here."

"What happens when you're better? Will you be somewhere I can come and see you?"

"Yes, they're sending me back to school. Mother wanted to send me to some place in Switzerland, but Higgy made her change her mind."

"Who's Higgy?"

"Miss Higgins, the headmistress. She said it would be a criminal waste of talent if I didn't go on."

"Well, you are rather brainy, I suppose, for a girl. That's good, then."

"I'm sorry, Paul," she says, "I haven't been out for so long, I'm getting cold already."

"The trot up the cliff will warm you," he says, taking her arm.

At the turn of the path they stop, and look out for a moment over beach and harbour and town, over the serenely restless sea, tossing and dreaming eternally in the great bight of the bay.

"I don't see what you meant just now, when you said it was too late, Madge, honest I don't," says Paul.

"Lucky you, Paul!" She turns her back on the wide view and walks slowly on. Behind her in the early lilac dusk the yellow light of Godrevy winks on. "Ralph said some things couldn't be mended, some things were too late to put right. And I just thought that sounded sick and wicked, I didn't understand what he meant at all. But now I see."